A Moore Affair

Michele Sims

Green Books Publishing

South Carolina

A Moore Affair by Michele Sims Copyright ©2020

Published by Green Books Publishing
Ebook ISBN: 978-1-7329031-6-6
Trade Paperback ISBN: 978-1-7329031-7-3

website: michelesims22.com

Cover Designed by: J.L Woodson: www.woodsoncreativestudio.com
Interior Designed by: Lissa Woodson: www.naleighnakai.com

Editor: TypeRight Editing

A Moore Affair

◆ DEDICATION ◆

Dedicated to my mother
and to all the women whom
have blessed me with their
love.

Chapter One

The perfect man. The perfect day. The perfect wedding. What could possibly go wrong? Especially after they took great pains to ensure that no one, including any of the groom's old flings would ruin their celebration in Scotland. Upon hearing that Bella was marrying Miles, some people weren't happy. However, she realized it wasn't her problem if others couldn't accept the inevitable. Tomorrow, she would become Mrs. Miles Moore.

Relax, girl. This is your time to shine.

Bella tried to reassure herself as she placed a hand above her knitted brow and sighed. Viewing the packed schedule for today, hours before her marriage to music sensation Miles "Ari" Moore, caused her heart to race with excitement and anxiety. The luxurious Middleton Resort ballroom in Glasgow buzzed with activity downstairs as the staff finished their final preparations for the facility's first big celebrity event.

Lunch buffet with Miles and his immediate family. Check.

Bridal party mani/pedis with champagne at the spa. Check.

A smile spread across her face as she peered at her French manicured nails and then lowered her head to look at her toenails, which were covered in a pearlescent polish, a light shade of blush.

Final meeting with wedding consultant. Check

Rehearsal dinner. Check.

Her phone vibrated and the name Mom flashed across the screen. Joan Wahlberg, her mother, a proud African American woman from Texas, had arrived in Scotland yesterday feeling the full effects of jetlag.

Before leaving her home, Joan had contacted the paternal side of Bella's family, the Campbell clan, whom she'd kept in touch with after John, her beloved husband and Bella's father, had died. Many members of John's family still lived in Scotland and were happy to hear of the upcoming nuptials of one of their relatives to a famous star and media mogul from the states. Fixing her gaze on the screen, Bella smiled at the image of her mother, who was staying in one of the rooms Bella had reserved for family members on the floor above her suite.

"Hello, Bella."

"Hello, Mom."

"Are you sure you don't want to come to the Campbell family get-together for a little while? They aren't expecting you to stay long, and the place they've rented isn't far from here."

"No, I think I'd better stay put." She looked at her nails as she spoke.

Loud claps of thunder could be heard in the distance, seconds before torrents of rain came down outside of her window.

"This storm wasn't predicted to be bad, and your cousin Colleen Campbell said that it should blow over quickly. Please honey, don't let the weather stop you from spending a little time with *your* family. Most of them haven't seen you since you were a little girl."

After warring with the idea of placing another event on her schedule, she decided against it, preferring to spend the time alone before the whirlwind of events tomorrow that would change her life forever.

"Mom, you know me, so you get that I do better when I've had some down time." She had retreated to her suite at the Middleton Resort for a much-needed break moments before Joan called. "Besides, I don't want to answer more questions about why Miles and I are rushing into marriage or hear superstitions about what it means if it rains on your wedding day. Is it good luck or bad luck? I've heard enough already." She sighed and saw her mother was frowning at her.

"People are curious, and I also had reservations about your quick decision to marry Miles weeks after you announced your engagement, but I came to the conclusion that it's your life and I won't stand in the way of your happiness. Sweetheart, I need to go and finish getting dressed if I'm to get there on time."

"Give them my regards, but before you go, I forgot to ask you about Mrs. Caspar. How is she doing?"

Mrs. Caspar had taken care of Bella when she was a child living in Texas.

"I saw her just before I left to come to Scotland, and you know her health has been failing, but she always found strength in her faith, and she was grateful for whatever time she had left. She sent her regards and told me to tell you that she loved you and prayed for your happiness. Several members from my side of the family are coming in tonight for the wedding, and let's be clear about something. I won't share with you any news I hear of Mrs. Caspar if she doesn't make it through the night, and our family members have strict orders not to mention it to you, so don't ask."

"Why not tell me? Is that another superstition that if someone you love dies on your wedding, it's bad luck?" Tears welled in her eyes.

"No, I don't believe in bad luck. A better question is why tell you if there's nothing you can do about it? Mrs. Caspar lived a full life, she was well-respected by others, and she loved you. That's all you need to remember about her on your wedding day. Honey, I really have to go."

"Alright Mom. I love you and have fun. Be careful out there."

"I will. Goodbye."

"Goodbye, Mom."

She ended the call and looked out the window, framed with its heavy ornate curtains drawn to the side. Before meeting Miles, she couldn't have imagined standing before a large picture window, watching nature's display of power and fury without hyperventilating. The rain, at times, was blinding, followed by bolts of lightning spreading across the sky illuminating the darkness. Just as suddenly as the rain had started to pour, drenching the landscape, there was an unexpected eerie stillness and calm as it subsided. Opening the door leading to her balcony, she smelled the ozone permeating the air as another line of storms made its way across the city of Glasgow. Her attention to the evening sky, with its dark clouds, was broken by the sound of her phone ringing again. She picked it up off the table and saw it was a call from Miles before she activated the speaker and video.

"Hey, babe. I needed to hear your voice."

"Hi, Miles. I thought you were preparing for your bachelor's party tonight."

"There's not much to prepare, and Parker, my dependable best man, has taken care of everything."

"Do you mean Parker, your partner in crime?" They shared lighthearted laughter, making the roar of the thunder and the cracks of lightning outside mere background noises.

"Is your mother with you?"

"No, she left to attend an event with my father's side of the family. Why are you really calling? Is there something I should know about?" Her heart rate quickened as she tried to brace herself for the news, good or bad.

"Nothing to worry about." His response was quick. "I was concerned about you, that's all."

She let out the breath she'd been holding and placed a hand on her chest.

"I'm fine," she assured him as she looked out the window. "Oh, I get it. You're worried I may be getting anxious because of the storms. Relax, storms haven't triggered me to have a panic attack in a year."

"I'm glad to hear it, but you also seemed bothered by something earlier today. You aren't getting cold feet about marrying me, are you?" His voice trailed off as he voiced his concerns.

"First of all, about the storms, my fears are replaced with memories of you being there and comforting me during one of the fiercest storms LA had ever seen. Aside from that, how could I be anxious when I was sitting near you lusting after your sexy body? That night was a game-changer for me."

She observed his shoulders relax as he smiled and laughed with her. It warmed her heart to see his gorgeous face looking back at her.

"About the wedding tomorrow—I can't wait to claim you as my man and become your wife."

"I'm glad to hear it and…can I come up to the suite just for a little while?"

"Miles, you know what's going to happen if you come."

"I know what I hope is going to happen. I need to make sure I'm not out of practice…you know, for the wedding night. Can you help a brother out?" He leaned into the camera, pleading with his eyes. "It has only been a few days since we last slept together. I promise I'll reward your sacrifice."

"I wasn't planning on sleeping, Bella."

"Go, and have fun with the guys tonight. I'm planning on turning in early and I'll see you tomorrow. I love you, Miles."

"I love you more. Sweet dreams and let them be about me and what I plan to do to you tomorrow."

Her core heated and became moist with anticipation as she imagined all he could do to excite her.

"I can't wait. Goodbye."

"Goodbye, my Bella."

She went to the drawer and grabbed a night shirt before heading to the shower and then off to bed.

* * *

Bella tossed in bed somewhere in the twilight of drowsiness as she descended into a deep sleep. Her body stilled as she focused her mind's eyes on an image of herself in a long white gown, the bottom of it wet and soiled with dirt as she stood before the image of a much younger Mrs. Caspar who looked back at her in silence.

"Am I rushing into marriage, Mrs. Caspar? Am I making a mistake?" Bella observed her image touching Mrs. Caspar's arms. "Please tell me?"

Bella waited for the answers, which, in her dream-like state, felt like an eternity. Instead of an answer, she saw a transformation of Mrs. Caspar growing older. Her plain nightgown, with its lack of adornment, changed into a beautiful wedding gown filled with jewels and a crown atop her head. The image of the older, wiser Mrs. Caspar finally spoke to her.

"Always remember, Bella, unto every life, a little rain must fall."

The image of Mrs. Caspar blurred as Bella, standing before her, wiped the tears from her eyes.

"Don't cry my child. You've always been loved, and you know what true love is and what it feels like. Don't let your fears stop you from embracing your truth."

Bella looked into the face of the woman who'd loved and cared for her dearly as a child.

"The truth is, I love Miles and he loves me. I'll never let anything come between us."

"No matter what, always remember your truth." Mrs. Caspar reminded her as she ascended high above her before she disappeared.

Bella awoke with tears on her pillow.

"Goodbye Mrs. Caspar, rest in peace. I love you," she whispered into the night as she slowly descended back to sleep, this time relaxed and at peace as she looked forward to becoming Miles's wife. She knew, loving Miles and having him love her until the end of time were her heart's greatest desires.

Nothing and no one would come between them.

Chapter Two

"I'm so glad the storms passed last night and this day is turning out to be gorgeous." Bella inhaled and thanked all that was good and benevolent in the universe as she sat in front of the balcony of her suite. Surveying the golden sunrays illuminating the lush wooded landscape still wet from the storms last night, she was grateful for this beautiful autumn day. The colors were vibrant and eye-catching as the leaves changed from green to fiery reds, orange, and yellow.

She pulled her robe around her shoulders and shivered, even though she had set the thermostat to keep the room comfortable. Just as she was about to get up, she looked down at the phone buzzing on the table beside the porcelain cup containing her morning tea.

Miles: *I love U Bella and soon I'll be your husband. I'm 1 lucky man.*

Bella: *I love you 2. I can't wait to be your wife.*

Replying to the text, she smiled at the image on the screen of her man as she walked to the seat at her dresser. Every nerve in her body had been tingling with excitement since she'd awoke early this morning, and the thought of him caused a wave of warmth and desire to flow throughout her body.

This was her wedding day.

Her mother sent a text earlier reminding her that she had spoken to the head of her Scottish clan, the Campbells, and he was happy to perform the duty of giving her away if it was what she desired. Instead, she reminded her mother she had thanked him personally, but she wanted them to walk down the aisle together as mother and daughter.

Showered in vanilla and lavender body wash and dressed in silk and lace undergarments under the silk robe she had purchased for her wedding, she sat by herself, wide awake, before calling Tina, her stylist, who had agreed to come to the renovated hospitality suite earlier than they'd planned, to do her hair and makeup. She was too excited to sleep. Tina had been highly recommended by the resort staff and had completed her task of making Bella bridal beautiful before Joan woke up.

Bella thanked Tina when she was finished and sat in front of her vanity mirror. She turned her head towards the sound of a knock on the door.

"Come in." She wondered if Tina had returned to get something she left in the room.

"Good morning, Bella." Her mother stood at the door before entering the room at a slow pace as if walking down a church aisle. Speechless, she stopped before she reached Bella.

"You—you look beautiful, sweetheart. Stunning. She really accentuated the beauty of your gorgeous brown eyes with that color palette." Joan looked at Bella's reflection in the mirror.

"Thank you. Tina is fantastic with makeup, and I'm pleased with the choices we made."

"I thought we scheduled Tina's appointment at this time so that she would be here when I arrived and I could watch her finish working her magic." Dressed in wedding attire with a matching clutch bag, her mother checked her watch as she walked into the room and placed a light kiss on Bella's smooth, brown cheek, being careful not to mess up her makeup.

"Good morning, Mom. I've been up for hours, so Tina agreed to come early." She patted her mother's hands and leaned into her embrace while they both looked at their reflection in the mirror and smiled.

"I see. It's probably just wedding day jitters, but don't worry. You're gorgeous, the wedding will go well, and Miles has already texted me to tell me good morning. He can be so thoughtful, and we're all going to have a great day." Joan gave Bella a big smile as she praised her soon to be son-in-law.

"Have you had something to eat dear? There's coffee and assorted items in the sitting area if you're hungry. I could get you something if you'd like."

"I'm too excited to eat, but I had a cup of tea earlier." She swallowed back emotions and rubbed her moist hands on her silk robe before she continued.

"I need to thank you for contacting our relatives to tell them about the wedding. I know it was short notice, and I'm grateful they'll be able to attend, but I'm sure I don't want our clan chief to walk me down the aisle, even though it's our family's tradition. The only man I would want to do that honor is… Daddy, and it's days like today I miss him so much." She choked on her words and looked in the mirror as she took a tissue her mother gave her to dry her eyes.

"I do, too; but I know he's here with us in our hearts. I feel his presence sending his blessings to you, Bella. You know how much he loved you, and I know he would have approved of your decision to marry Miles, despite my initial concerns. Miles has proven to me he loves you, and I give you both my full blessings." She stood behind her daughter and gave her a hug around the shoulders before straightening Bella's veil.

"Don't go messing up your makeup with tears. I need you to turn your head so I can tighten a few pins in your hair."

Bella dried her eyes, turned her head to the side, and looked in the mirror at her mother, who was distracting herself by curling Bella's tendril curls with her fingers and smoothing her hair, although Tina had finished styling it and pinning on her veil minutes ago. She knew this day had to be hard on her mother, too. She reached back and patted her mother's hand as she fussed over her hair.

"There, I'm done. We don't want the hair pins to fall out." After she finished securing the pins, Joan retrieved the clutch bag she had placed on the vanity and pulled out a string of pearls.

"These are my mother's pearls, and I wore them on my wedding day. I'm proud I can give them to you, and they will look lovely with your dress." Joan smiled as she fastened the pearls around Bella's neck.

"I agree, and thank you for such a wonderful gift." She ran her fingers along the smooth, silky white pearls.

"Let me help you into your dress." Bella got up, joined her mother in front of her dress hanging in the corner, and took it off the silk hanger.

"I love you, Mom." Bella stood in front of her mother as she helped her into her dress.

"I love you, too. You're a lovely bride, my sweet girl." Joan smoothed out the dress after fastening the last closure, and they looked in the mirror one last time.

"Let's go out and join the rest of the bridal party before they get concerned you're having cold feet." She smiled at Bella.

"I'm giddy, but no cold feet here, Mom. I'm looking forward to claiming my man, but there is one thing I need to tell you so you won't worry someone will break the news to me."

"What is it?" Her mother's eyes widened with concern, which Bella sensed was a confirmation of her dream from last night.

"I know Mrs. Caspar is no longer here. I felt her spirit as she passed."

Her mother's eyes glistened as she swallowed hard. "The two of you always had a strong connection to each other from the time you were a child, but tell me, who told you?" Joan's chest heaved in anger and Bella came closer to embrace her.

"No one told me, I just knew. Don't worry, Mom. I have wonderful memories of her, and I feel it's going to be alright. As you said, she lived a wonderful life, and I plan to fully embrace life as she did."

"Are you really alright?" Joan looked into Bella eyes, searching for the truth, and smiled.

"Yes, I am." She nodded as she touched her mother's cheek.

"Alright, let's get you married."

"Yes, Mom; let's do it." They hugged and then gathered their things before leaving the inner dressing room.

* * *

Jen Middleton, Parker's wife, Reagan Madison, one of her besties, and NeNe Moore, Miles's cousin, were her bridesmaids. Darien Grayson, Miles's executive assistant and also her bestie, had agreed to be her man of honor. The wedding was to be held in the harbor on one of the few remaining large historic ships.

Sean, her wedding director, gasped as she entered the outer room. "Oh, Bella. You're a beautiful bride, as I knew you would be."

"Thank you, Sean." Her cheeks warmed as she took in the compliment.

She *was* a beautiful bride, in her white flowing gown fitted to her svelte shape. Although she once thought she would be draped in puffy formal wedding attire custom made for a princess, with yards of fabric complete with a long majestic train, she'd decided she really didn't want to fuss over a dress all night that hindered her movements. Instead, she chose a dress of simplistic elegance that fit her close and flattered her curvy figure. She wore a V-neck halter floor-length dress with crossing details at the bodice made of posh chiffon covering French silk.

"Here's your bouquet, Bella." Sean handed her the ball of white and blush flowers tied together with a ribbon in a bow. A small piece of her clan's tartan was placed inside the bouquet she would carry down the aisle in front of her, near her heart.

"Miles and members of the bridal party have already left for the ship, and he's anxiously waiting for you there. That lad is in love, and I don't think I've seen a man as excited as he is to get married in a long time."

"We're lucky to have each other, Sean," Bella told him while Joan nodded in agreement.

"We'd better get going," he urged her as she hooked her arm around his before he escorted her and Joan to the limousine waiting out front to take them to the ceremony. Several of the guests at the resort offered up well wishes and comments about her beautiful dress as she passed through the lobby, surrounded by members of security. Joan entered the car first, followed by Bella, who needed more help from staff to get in the limo without wrinkling her dress. The driver, Jaimie MacGregor, started the car and, instead of the short ride they anticipated, their convoy of limos with members of security in front and behind her car were caught in a traffic jam, with no way to escape the long line of vehicles snaking their way through the busy streets.

"There's a bad accident up ahead," Jaimie informed them after fifteen minutes of sitting in traffic going nowhere.

"Thanks for letting us know." Bella sat back in her seat, remaining as calm as she could while her mother patted her hand.

"Don't worry, sweetheart. It's going to be alright." Joan spoke as if needing to dispel her fears.

"I'm not worried Mom. Miles loves me, and I know he'll be waiting for me." She smoothed out her dress and looked at her bouquet of flowers with a resolve that nothing would ruin her day.

"Bella, we know an alternate route, but it may get bumpy at times. Hold on, okay? We'll get you to the ceremony on time," Jaimie told her, looking over his shoulder.

"Fine, do what you need to do." Her heart was beating hard despite her attempts to outwardly remain calm. Instrumental music streaming in the back of the limo was drowned out by Jaimie laying on his horn to alert the drivers in the next lane the convoy was coming over. Abruptly, he turned the car onto a side street, causing Joan and Bella's shoulders to jerk and sway in their seats as they held on.

"Oh my gosh!" Joan screamed out, just as another car came out of nowhere, clipping the back bumper and causing the car to fishtail before Jaimie regained control and avoided slamming into a car in front of him.

"Are you alright?" Bella reached out to Joan.

"Yes. I'm okay," she replied breathlessly.

"I got this, ladies. You're safe with me."

"Safe?" Bella looked at Joan and grabbed her hand before they both slumped into the seat.

They looked out the back window at the cars behind them, some of which were caught up in a mangled mess of fender-benders.

"Don't worry. I'll check on the guys after I get you to the ceremony." Jaimie sped away from the mess as police cars with red lights and sirens blaring raced past them.

They finally arrived at the dock after a ride that would have frayed anyone's nerves, not just a bride on her wedding day.

"We're here." Joan spoke with a sense of relief as she caught her breath.

"And in one piece." Bella let out a deep breath.

"Can we sit for a few minutes before we go inside? I need a little time to gather my wits." Joan massaged the back of her neck, which was tense after their unexpected detour.

"Sure, Mom; but not for too long. I don't want Miles to worry about us." She leaned forward to look out the window at the guests still arriving at the dock.

"Bella—"

Bella waved away her mother's concerns.

"I'm sure, Mom. This is what I want, and now, more than ever. I want to become Miles's wife." They held hands and bowed their heads as a silent prayer passing between them melted away the doubts.

Jaimie came and opened the door to assist as the staff from the ship appeared alongside the car to help them to the top of the private gangway, where her bridal party awaited them on deck. The ship's quartermaster blew his whistle, announcing Bella's arrival as she walked to the area outside of the chapel, and each member of the wedding party hugged her just before they gathered to walk down the aisle.

"Oh Bella. You're beautiful." Bella beamed as her wedding party gasped and offered her hugs and compliments, while Sean encouraged them to get in line before the ceremony started.

Bella watched as each of her bridesmaids entered the room, and then it was her turn. Her lightweight fabric gave her the appearance of floating down the aisle as she took small graceful steps toward her groom, waiting for her at the altar decorated with white- and blush-colored flowers matching the ones in her bouquet. The sounds from a musical trio composed of a bagpipe, a violin, and a drum filled the room while she and her mother took their steps to the altar.

Miles, handsome in a black custom tuxedo, cast his gaze upon her with bright eyes and a wide smile as she entered the room. He kept his hands behind his back, and she smiled as he rocked on his heels. She knew he did that when he was trying to contain his excitement.

It delighted her to see a rare view of the bubbly, effervescent side of his personality. They exchanged smiles as she made her way to him. His display of happiness was contagious and calmed her nerves.

"Glad to see you've arrived," he whispered into her ear after she and Joan made their way up the aisle.

"There's no other place on earth I'd rather be." She looked into his eyes and touched the side of his cheek.

The Campbell Laird had presented Bella with a tartan blanket monogrammed with the Campbell clan's motto—*Forget Not*—at the family brunch a day before the wedding, and he proudly displayed it at the entrance of the room, hung on an ornate metal stand. She would never forget her father, and she felt his presence on her special day.

She always thought of herself as a "daddy's girl," but Miles told her days before their wedding she was like her mother: strong, determined, and capable of a deep, abiding, lifelong love. She loved Miles Moore, and she thought herself the luckiest woman in the world.

Her mother announced that she offered her daughter in marriage, then took her seat before Bella turned to face Miles.

The room overflowed with members of the Moore family who had come to Scotland the day before the ceremony to witness their nuptials and share their excitement in adding another member to the family.

"Do you take this woman to be your wife, to love, honor, and cherish her until death do you part?" She looked up at the officiant and then at Miles.

"I do." His answer, loud and resolute, startled her and caused their audience of well-wishers to fill the room with laughter.

"Do you take this man to be your husband, to love, honor, and cherish him until death do you part?" the officiant asked. Their hands joined, and with tears glistening her eyes, she responded.

"I do, with all my heart."

They exchanged rings, and she felt him place an eager hand at the back of her head and guide it close to his. He kissed her long and hard before the officiant finished pronouncing them married.

Her face warmed with heat, and her heart swelled with joy. She'd never been happier in her life, and they turned, facing the room filled with family and friends for the first time as a married couple before walking down the aisle showered with the petals of white and blush pink roses. The wedding party assembled in front of the limo, waiting to take the happy couple to the reception at the resort to surprise them with a shower of pink and red roses to symbolize the joining of their hearts with their favorite colors.

Chapter Three

The reception was a regal affair in the ballroom, filled with crystal chandeliers hanging from the ceiling and floral arrangements in large brilliant vases that reflected light from the collections of candles throughout the romantic space. They had a little time alone together before their presentation to their guests, since Miles had insisted they dispense with a receiving line. He wanted to take pictures, mingle, and start the honeymoon as soon as possible.

"Sweetheart, don't forget we agreed to give an exclusive of our reception photos to my friend Charlie for the first publication in his magazine. We must pose for the obligatory cake-cutting pictures, dance pictures, and…you know the routine."

"I'll keep my part of the bargain, but let's keep it short. I have plans for you." He held her hand and reached over to kiss her on the lips before walking the short distance to the front of the ballroom.

"I present to you Mr. Miles Aridio Tavares Moore and Mrs. Bella Aliyah Wahlberg Moore," they heard the announcer tell the guests gathered for their opulent affair.

"Showtime," he announced to her as she watched him plaster on his Ari smile, the one he used on stage when he performed at his mega hip-hop concerts. She began to wonder for the first time if having the media involved in their special day was a good idea. She planned to spend her life with Miles, an authentic man, not some highly marketed hip-hop star, so she brushed away her slight bristle, smiled, and walked into the room with her husband ensconced in his Ari persona.

* * *

Over an hour had passed since the start of their reception, and he kept his part of the bargain, smiling his Ari smile when he needed to, posing with young members of the Campbell clan to take pictures, and signing autographs. He even gave his raucous laugh for media consumption at jokes she knew in reality he probably didn't think were funny. Miles stayed hidden under the mask he wore when he was working the crowd, and it saddened her. Their special day was disintegrating into a well-crafted affair for the media instead of an intimate gathering of family and friends. She smiled, happy she had married the man of her dreams, but she realized he wouldn't be happy spending his life in a bubble, hiding his true self and possibly disconnecting from the fun-loving Miles she had grown to love.

Maybe it's why he spent so much time away from others after his tours ended, chasing volcanoes and surrounded by nature. He needed time away from the cameras and the constant gaze of others in order not to lose himself.

They stayed at each other's side, greeting guests and taking part in planned activities coordinated by their reception director. Several executives from other companies in the music industry had come to Scotland and were present. They came forward to offer congratulations, and despite reminding him she had met several of them in California, he introduced her as if they were meeting her for the first time.

"Miles, Miles!" Bella looked back at Mya Kelly, a middle-aged woman waving and dressed in a tight gold dress. Bella knew she was the owner of Kelly Music Productions and a few other things. Pushing members of the wait staff carrying heavy trays as she made her way through the crowd, Mya was focused on getting Miles's attention.

"Shit. What is she doing here?" he cursed under his breath and rolled his eyes.

Bella wondered the same thing, as she had reviewed the guest list several times and knew all the invited guests. Mya picked up her pace and almost galloped toward them as Miles pulled Bella in the opposite direction, acting as if he didn't hear her calling him.

"Miles Moore, I'm trying to congratulate you and I've traveled a long way to do so." She caught up with them and pulled him into an embrace as he stood tall, like a wooden figure in front of her, refusing to let go of Bella's hand.

"Thank you, Mya. I thought you were too busy running your company to come to this affair." He gave her a slight smile, devoid of genuine emotion.

"Oh, and is that why I had to catch up with your mother to get one of the invitations you gave her for family and close friends? You know we Kellys and Moores go way back."

Mya kept her attention on Miles as Bella observed their awkward exchange.

"Maybe we could discuss a music venture between our two companies before you leave Scotland, maybe tomorrow?"

"Mya, excuse me if I remind you of the obvious but…," he pinched the bridge of his nose, "Bella and I just got married, and we'll be starting our honeymoon soon. I'm sure you didn't mean to slight her by failing to acknowledge her presence as my bride on our wedding day." He kissed the back of Bella's hand, exposing her freshly manicured nails.

Like hell she didn't. Bella gave Mya a ghost of a smile, mirroring the one Miles was wearing.

"Forgive me. Of course I meant to extend my congratulations to you too, Bella. Didn't we meet at an event months ago? You're Miles's media consultant, aren't you?"

"Among other things. Mya, and now, excuse us please."

Miles responded as Bella returned a wave and smiled at one of the other guests.

"This isn't cool, Mya." He frowned; his remarks curt.

"I didn't mean to offend." She leaned away from him.

"As I said, this is our wedding day, and it's all about us enjoying our special day, so if you'll excuse us, we need to speak to other guests before we leave." He turned away, leaving her standing alone as she took a glass of champagne from a waiter passing by while he and Bella greeted other guests.

"Well, that was interesting, to say the least." The smile across Bella's face brightened, but her words dripped with sarcasm. She had heard rumors through back channels that Mya had an affair with Miles while she was still with her husband. Shaking her head, she tried ridding herself of the image of Miles with Mya but she couldn't.

"Is there something I should know about you and Mya?" She looked up at him and arched an eyebrow letting him know she already knew something about their sordid past.

He broke eye contact for a second and turned his head.

"No, nothing that matters on our wedding day, but she did make me realize that some of the music execs know you as my former media consultant for AriMusic. I need to make sure they know I expect you to have all the respect, rights, and privileges of being my wife and my business partner. I'll not tolerate them refusing to treat you as my equal."

Not the answer I expected but it will have to do for now. She pondered and accepted his decision to change the subject.

"Thank you, but they already know how you feel about things, and I'm sure they won't intentionally disrespect me as your wife. The men here aren't interested in getting in your pants." She laughed as he tightened his grip on her hand while she spoke to him.

"I'm not concerned about the others, and I'm thankful you were clear with Mya. I know a female in heat when I see one, and Mya still has the hots for you."

"Enough about her." He frowned and shook his head as she looked over and saw Reagan and NeNe standing near the bar.

"I'll be right back, Miles. I need to talk with Reagan and NeNe."

"Don't be gone too long. I have plans for us." He smiled and she kissed him before walking across the room, where members of the wedding party had congregated. Looking back at him, she saw him grab another glass of fine Champagne off the waiter's tray. With a quick glance around the room, she was happy Mya was nowhere in sight.

Mya has left the building, she thought to herself. *I know my man, and when he's in the public eye, he drinks Champagne or French wine at media gatherings, but he prefers a glass of good Scotch when he's really enjoying himself. I need to do something.*

She hoped an idea would come to her. She saw him interacting with a photographer, and he seemed angry about something, though she couldn't hear the words they exchanged as she crossed the room to talk to Reagan and NeNe.

"Reagan, I need your help to change my clothes. Will you join me in the dressing room in say thirty or thirty-five minutes? Knock before you enter the room. I'll be there waiting for you. NeNe, can you come with Reagan and take Miles back to the reception while I get dressed? I need you to shadow him. I think he's getting the same hemmed-in feeling he experiences when I let the meet and greets last longer than two hours."

"Sure," they told her in unison.

"Thank you, now let me return to my husband."

People approaching and wanting to take pictures with her slowed her attempt to return to his side. Before she made it over to him, she beckoned to a member of the reception staff so she could have a waiter place a glass of scotch in their dressing room.

He deserves it and will probably need it about now.

She finally reached him and took him by the hand to guide him out of the ballroom.

"Are we getting out of here?"

"Not yet," she advised him and took the glass of Champagne out of his hand, placing it on the tray of another waiter standing nearby.

"Shit. What's left for us to do?"

"Enjoy our guests," she responded. They steadily made their way out of the room while remembering to smile at others as they departed. They arrived in the dressing room set up just for them, and she locked the door behind her. Spotting the glass of scotch on the table to the side of the room, she went to pick it up before joining him in the center of the room. She held onto the glass and turned around, her back to him.

"Unzip my dress, please. I need help to get out of it." He came forward and kissed her on the shoulder before taking her zipper into his hand. She felt the warmth of his hands, and the feel of his lips descending her back sent tingles down her spine. The metal grinding sound of the zipper drifting down her back excited her, heightening her tensions with anticipation of what was to come.

"That's more like it, baby. Just me and you and our bodies entwined in love."

He moved in closer to her, his chest to her back, and placed his hand low on her belly to pull her close, his shaft hardening and pressed against her buttocks. He grinded against her for a few moments, but she pulled away after he removed her dress one shoulder at a time. She stepped out of the dress but kept on her stiletto heels and turned around, handing him the glass of scotch.

He took one quick sip and placed it on a table nearby while she stood close to him, watching him tear his clothes off and step out of his shoes. He smiled, standing in front of her naked. She had tried on several types of underwear before the wedding, and she could tell by looking at his slackened jaw and wide eyes that she'd made the right choice of a white strapless corset of silk tied up with satin ribbons running down its front with a matching white laced silk thong. She had her veil attached to her hair with a small tiara hanging below her shoulders, and she placed her hand on her head to take it off but was stopped by his first utterings since she'd stepped out of her dress.

"Don't take off the veil and don't take the pins out of your hair. I want to do that myself. I've dreamed of laying your body before me on sheets of satin to adore you before I claim you for the first time as my wife. You're mine, baby."

He stroked himself as he moved closer to her.

"There's no bed in here, but I can't wait. I need you now. I'll enjoy my fantasy later."

He came to her and looked at her, loosening the ribbons and hooks on the corset. She felt his warm breath on the mounds of breast and saw his chest heave at a quick pace as he remained close, waiting for her to free her body from the material wrapped around her chest. She took off the corset, but before she could remove her panties, he took her up into his arms, moving quickly toward the vanity, and kicked the small chair in front of the vanity to the side, placing her on top of the dresser. The skin of her back felt cool against the similar mirror she had gazed into before their wedding. She placed her arms around his neck and opened her legs, allowing him full access to her core. She wanted him as much as he needed to have her right now.

"I'm going to take you hard. I promise to take my time and make it sweeter later, but I need to have you now." His breath quickened as he spoke. He moved her thong to the side before he quickly entered her, but he cradled her buttocks to stop her body from slamming against the mirror. She felt small trickles of sweat dripping from his body onto hers, cooling their mutual fires before their heightened excitement burst with unbridled passion.

"You drive me crazy with desire. I love you, Bella. I love you so much," he panted.

"I love you too." Her breath quickened as she struggled to get out the words before exploding into an orgasmic haze. He placed his forehead to hers after finding his release while she kept her legs wrapped around him, still feeling him throbbing inside her. Smiling, she enjoyed the warmth of his forehead touching hers, and he smiled back, kissing her lovingly on the cheeks as they remained joined for several moments.

"Now that's the way to start a honeymoon. Let's grab our clothes and make a break for it. We can continue what we started in our room upstairs. You gave me an appetizer, and now it's my turn to serve up a complete multi-course meal." He winked at her and offered his help to get her down from the vanity table.

"We can't ghost on our guests. They've traveled many miles at great time and expense to be with us today. I thought we could have a quickie, settle you down, and then go out to enjoy the festivities. We've posed for all the pictures we agreed to, and now it's our turn to have some fun."

"There's no disagreement here. It is our turn for a little fun, and I plan to spend it with you in our bedroom." She grabbed a towel and tossed it to him before heading to the clothes rack in the corner and grabbing a change of clothing for him.

"Why don't you freshen up and then slip on these things I had placed in the room for you. You purchased a trousseau for me, and I had custom-made Italian shirts and tailored pants made for you. They feel great and are more comfortable than your tuxedo." She rubbed her hands across the material and held up the outfit for him to see, but he didn't come forward.

"I'm ready to leave now. I want some time alone with my wife."

She placed the clothes back on the rack, sauntered toward him, and pressed her body close to his.

"Baby, we can't just leave. It's not how we do things." She pulled his head down and kissed his furrowed brow and his tightened lips until they loosened.

"I promise I'll make it worth the wait. Please do this for me. I have a surprise waiting for you."

"What kind of surprise?" His frown softened as she touched him with her lips against his cheeks and on his chest.

"Don't make me ruin the surprise." They both turned their heads to the sound of light knocks on the door.

"Bella, it's us, Reagan and NeNe."

"Just a minute." She loosened herself from his embrace and went to the clothing rack, grabbed her robe, and tied it around her.

"Miles, go behind the privacy screen in the corner and get dressed." He went to the rack and got his new outfit while she scampered to the vanity drawer containing fresh underwear for them both. He took his time getting behind the decorative panels in the room's corner.

"I'll be right there," she called out.

"You always think of everything, Bella." He grabbed his underwear and body wipes to freshen up.

"I always have a change of clothes available for you when we attend events." *I can't believe I'm comparing my reception to a media event.*

She shook her head.

"Hurry, Miles. We'll have our couple's dance, and we can leave right after my surprise to you, if you wish. I promise." She had to admit their wedding was turning into a media event, something he didn't want to happen. He came from behind the panel clad in his shirt and pants.

"I love the view, you handsome devil." She looked back, went to the door, and opened it. Reagan and NeNe had their hands on their hips.

"Are we interrupting anything, Bella?" NeNe asked, pointing to their wedding attire puddled on the floor.

"No, you're not," she pulled her robe close to her neck and tightened the belt around her waist. "You're just in time. Can you and my handsome husband entertain our guests while Reagan helps me change into my dress?"

She went to him and straightened out his shirt, so it fell just right on his shoulders. As she helped him finish buttoning it, she looked into his eyes while she tucked the tail of it into his pants, lightly touching his happy trail.

"You're so bad, Bella." He smiled at her. "Hurry up and remember your promise. I plan to hold you to it." He kissed her on the nose and grabbed his glass of scotch before departing from the room with NeNe.

She grabbed their clothes off the floor and placed them in a chair before going behind the panel to freshen up.

"My dress is hanging in the corner. Can you get it for me? I'll need help fastening the pearl buttons in the back of dress." Reagan nodded and walked to the corner to get the dress.

Her form-fitting dress made of lace and silk was sleeveless, with a high, rounded neckline. She'd had it hemmed to hit above her knees, allowing enough fabric to provide her with modesty and a covering of her ample buttocks when she bent over. The back was cut out just above the small of her back, revealing her smooth brown skin.

"Girl, I'm nervous. I don't know if I'll remember all the steps to the routine. I thought it was a good idea to use one of his songs for our first dance, but I'm not sure about it now." She shimmied into the tight-fitting dress while sharing her fears.

"Don't worry about it. You can do a regular slow dance to the song if you don't want to do the routine we've practiced many times. You've got this, girl. Turn around so I can finish buttoning your dress."

She turned and faced the mirror to visualize herself performing the dance routine.

Hands on his shoulder, exaggerate hip action, walk around in a circle.

"Please be still while I finish buttoning your dress. Do you want me to help you take your hair down?"

"No, Miles will freak if I take my hair down. He wants to do it later tonight."

"He's such a romantic with you." Bella cocked her head to the side and looked at Reagan in the mirror.

"What do you mean with me?"

"Bella, it's nothing you probably don't already know. You're aware I've been with his company for quite some time, and I've seen women come and go in Miles's life. It's just when he was with the others, he never did the flowers and candles thing. I always thought it was one of his major shortcomings. Before you, he never seemed to understand what it was like to cherish a woman. You know, romance her a little."

"Yes, I need romance, and you know what? I think he enjoys the romance in our relationship too." She looked at herself one last time. "I think I'm ready. Thanks for your help." She turned and offered Reagan a warm hug. "I'll join you after I alert the room attendant to gather our clothes and take them to the honeymoon suite. I'll be out shortly."

"Sure, let's have some fun. It's your special day, not a public performance. I'm a professional dancer, and I forget a few steps sometimes. Laugh it off, girl." She hugged her again before leaving the room.

Bella walked back to the ballroom, accompanied by a member of security who was waiting for her just outside the door of the dressing room. She joined Miles, who was talking to her mother and Charlie.

"You look lovely, my sweet girl. Why didn't you tell me you planned to change your dress? I would have helped you."

"Thanks, Mom, but Reagan helped me."

"Yes, your dress is lovely," Charlie agreed. "The affair this evening was wonderful. We already have great shots of the reception, and I must leave to get the article completed for print as soon as possible, but I wanted to say good night before I left with my crew. I thank you both for the exclusive."

He came forward, and she turned her head, allowing him to plant a kiss on her cheek. "Good bye, Charlie; thanks for coming."

"My blessing to the two of you for a happy and long union," he offered before leaving the ballroom and waving goodbye.

They waved goodbye to Charlie, and she waited a bit before giving a thumb's up to the bandleader and Reagan standing nearby with a few of the dancers.

"I've cued the music. Mom, will you excuse us while we have our first dance as husband and wife?"

"Sure, dear. I'll go back to my table. I just came over to say good night to Charlie before he left."

She took Miles by the hand and led him to the middle of the dance floor.

"You're one gorgeous bride. I love both of your dress choices." He took her into his arms and awaited the start of the music. It surprised him she chose one of his songs, "My North Star." The lights went down except for a spotlight on them, and the band played the instrumental version of the song.

She'd had Reagan help her change a few of the steps in the routine. She wasn't trying to recapture the magical moment he'd had on stage with a dancer during his tour a year ago, but she loved the lyrics of the song and wanted to make their dance as special and unique as their love was. She turned her back to his side and shimmied down the length of his body to the music and then faced him, as they joined hands, moving to the beat of the music. He smiled, urging her on and encouraging her to move as if no one was watching.

"You're doing it, girl. Love the way you move."

She kept a hand on his shoulders and walked around him, displaying the back of her dress as she encircled him. Shaking her shoulders sensually, she returned to face him to the beat of the music, and he placed his hands on her waist while she leaned back, their groins in contact. He supported her weight as they twirled in a circle and grabbed her back, allowing her to pull her body up. She placed her hands around his neck in time for the chorus to the song, and he motioned for someone in technical support to give him a mic. The guy ran full speed to him with a mic and disappeared quickly from the floor, as if always in tune to his requests. She had never sung in front of him or in public before, but she smiled and joined him in singing the last verse and the chorus.

You're my guide
I'm lost without you by my side
My passions burn for you
I'll always yearn to be with you
Illuminating the darkness of night
Shining ever so bright
My beautiful shining light

I'll always return to you
Whether near or far
I love the person you are
You're my North Star

The spotlights went down, and they stood in the middle of the floor, kissing to the applause and cheers of their guests. He kept his forehead to hers as she let out a breath of relief, glad it was over. He motioned for the lights to come back up and joined their guests in applauding her before leading the way to their sweetheart table to sit down and let her catch her breath. She held her hand to her heart, which was beating wildly, and took deep breaths as they made their way across the floor.

"I didn't know you could sing. I've never heard you sing before."

"A woman should always keep a few things to herself to the surprise of those who think they know her well. I wasn't planning on singing tonight. It just seemed like the right thing to do. You made me feel so comfortable, as if it was just the two of us out there."

She looked over the audience and saw her mother wipe a tear away and blow kisses their way as she waved back at her and to Miles's parents standing nearby. They reached the table, and he pulled out her seat while signaling a waiter to come over and freshen their glasses with iced water. Taking her glass from the waiter, she drank most of the contents, and declined the offer for wine or more alcohol.

"I'll have another scotch," Miles requested, and he leaned over to whisper to her.

"Thank you. I loved the surprise. I didn't want to burden you with my family's tradition of having the bride dance for her groom. I thought it would make you uncomfortable being the center of attention."

"Your mother told me about the tradition, but I was already planning on doing something like a dance with you, not necessarily for you. I chose to be a part of a family of entertainers, and being in the spotlight comes with the territory. I have to admit it was frightening and exhilarating, but fun once I settled down and let myself enjoy it."

"You're a natural."

The waiter returned and gave him the glass of scotch. He took a sip and got the attention of the same tech guy, who ran toward him with a guitar in his hand and a mic headset.

"It's my turn to salute my bride," he spoke into the mic. He fastened it on his head and took the guitar from the guy, who scooted back to his position near the band. Miles placed the strap of the guitar across his shoulder and played a chord.

After Miles instructed the band, they struck up the music for a medley of love songs, and he began playing his guitar as the instrumental soloist. Toward the end of the medley, he sang her favorite verse from one of his popular songs.

Your beauty transcends my sight
I see you with my heart
I feel you in my soul

My love for you
will never grow old
I'm blessed you're mine
I'll love you for all time
Until the end of time

Their guests applauded again after he finished his tribute to her and returned to their table. Rising from her seat, she wrapped her arms around his neck, planting quick kisses on his lips as a red flush spread across his cheeks. He gave her the sexiest, most boyish grin she had ever seen as she gazed at him in admiration, and warm thoughts crossed her mind.

He's so talented and I love him so much.

"That was beautiful. I feel like the luckiest girl in the world, and I'll never forget this moment as long as I live." She smiled, pressing her forehead to his. He pushed his guitar out of the way and tightened their embrace.

"Are you ready to go? I plan to keep my promise to you," she reminded him.

"I was about to ask you about leaving. You know I was ready an hour ago. We can make our way around the room saying goodbye to everyone and then you're all mine."

He took her by the hand and directed their path around the ballroom with the band playing in the background. Some guests danced while others waited patiently for the young couple to make their way to their table for a quick chat before they departed the room. His parents assured them they would take over hosting the party, and she hugged her mother one last time. She saw Miles look toward the exit just as he grabbed her hand and hurried her out of the room toward the nearest elevator to their penthouse suite.

A member of security strode beside them to the elevator, up to their floor, and out of the elevator to plant himself alongside another employee already seated in the alcove of their exclusive floor. Bella looked around at the level of security while Miles guided her to the door, leading to a more private area, and opened it before picking her up and taking her across the threshold.

One of the security guards closed the door behind them as Miles took Bella to the bedroom, which was filled with flowers and lighted long tapered candles, some in hurricane vases, located around the room. Placing her on her feet, he kissed her and immediately unbuttoned his shirt as she looked on, her jaw slackened as she watched him.

"Wait!" She held up her hand as he looked at her with his fingers still on the third button on his shirt.

"What? Things were just starting to get interesting."

She sauntered closer to him and placed her hands over his as she planted a kiss on his lips.

"Why do we need so much security around us? Have there been additional threats against you since the end of the Fire God Tour?"

"No, there hasn't been, but I need to know you're safe at all times. That reminds me. I haven't had a chance to talk to you about this morning. Why were you late?"

"We got caught in traffic, and Jaimie, your professional driver that could have been a stunt man in any action film, took us along a different route."

"Oh, I'm glad it wasn't something else."

"Like what Miles? I'm serious. I know I just agreed to be a part of your life for better or worse, but I'm not signing on to having every aspect of my life observed by others. I'm not willing to live in a fishbowl surrounded by security, and really Miles, you know I love you, but having me and my mother come to the ceremony in a convoy like we were some group of dignitaries or heads of state only called more attention to us."

"I see your point, and I'll reduce your security detail."

"Get rid of my security detail, Miles." She floated the idea as she pressed her body close to his and placed her arms around his neck, brushing her lips against his.

"You're not playing fair, and you know you can get anything out of me when I'm horny as hell."

"So, no more security?" She batted her eyelashes at him.

"I'll get rid of the security guys for you I've retained and I'll talk to the people at the Network and tell them to back off, but I can't promise anything when it comes to them. My family has been affiliated with them since before I was born, and no one tells the Network what to do."

Miles's father Cade and his Uncle Vincent were secret operatives with The Network, an international, highly organized intelligence group of agents and operatives where people of power, politicians, military leaders, captains of industry, mercenary soldiers, and people from all walks of life came together to achieve mutual goals.

"I can live with that for now." She helped him unbutton his shirt.

"Good. Let's not waste any more time talking about security."

"I agree, but first help me get out of my dress." She turned around, her back to him to get assistance with her buttons. She looked over her shoulder, curious why he was silent and not helping her.

"Is there something wrong?"

"No, I realize how beautiful this moment is for us, and I don't want to rush it."

He took the tiara attached to her veil out of her hair and set it on a table. Placing his hand on her first button, he loosened it and kissed her back every time he loosened two buttons until her back was completely exposed.

"You're so beautiful, and I'm a lucky man to call you my wife." He pushed the dress over her shoulders after loosening all the buttons and pulled down the zipper holding the dress together from the small of her back, past her buttocks. She heard him take in a breath after he exposed her strapless bra and lace high-cut bikini panties. She stepped out of her dress and turned around.

With a lidded gaze, he surveyed her body, from her head to her breasts, down to her panties and to her pedicured feet in stiletto heels. She crossed her arms and shielded her breasts, surprised by her discomfort under his unwavering attention as he moved in closer to her.

"Don't be shy. I'm admiring your beautiful body and fantasizing what I plan to do with it."

"It's your turn to take off your clothes. Remind me what you got big boy."

She moved to the bed to watch him first take off his shirt before pulling at the zipper to loosen his pants. The brilliant glow from the candles provided an aura around his naked body and reflected light off the platinum wedding band and the white gold chain, with its etched ram's head pendant around his neck. He saw a brush with a silver handle on the table, took it in his hands, and sauntered to her as she licked her lips hungry for his touch and the feel of him inside her.

"This isn't the time to play hairdresser. Stop taunting me and take me now." Her head fell back, and she rolled her eyes.

"Patience, baby. Let our lovemaking unfold organically. I'm enjoying this time together and I've waited for it all day." He moved closer to her and threw one of his legs behind her, placing her between his legs and causing his erection to press against her buttocks.

"I want to loosen your hair first, and I'm getting harder just thinking about it."

She pressed her eyes shut.

Give me strength to remember how much I love this man. She sighed, giving in to his desire.

"All right, baby, I'm all yours." Electric shocks tingled down her spine and she shivered from the feel of his nimble fingers working their way through her hair and removing the pins that held her hair in a tight bun. Her hair fell to her shoulders as he located most of the pins and massaged her scalp. She turned her head, exposing the skin on her neck, heating up from his breath and the kisses he placed all the way to her shoulders. He massaged her breasts in circular movements and, with joined hands low around her hips, grinded against her as he whispered words of love in her ear.

"Take me. Now. You've got me excited. I need relief," she panted.

"Surrender to me, and I'll give you the release you're craving. I promise."

"No more foreplay. I need you now." She got up, pushed him down on the bed, and straddled him. "This cowgirl is taking what she needs."

She ran her hands along the planes of his toned chest, feeling the muscles drawn taut and tense under the feel of her hand. She sensed her power as he surrendered to her, his shaft ready for her as he watched her, in silence, position herself over him and guide him inside before riding him as hard as she could.

She released a deep breath, the pitch of her sexual tension easing as she gyrated her hips.

"Take your time, baby; your pleasure is my pleasure. I'm here for you and loving my badass girl taking charge. This feels so good."

He grabbed her thighs, and she smiled as he lay back to enjoy the visual and physical pleasures of their lovemaking. Their breaths quickened, and she cast her gaze on his chest, sweating and heaving with pleasure. He continued thrusting inside her, and his face contorted in a crescendo of mounting tension until he yelled out.

"Oh, Bella. Oh, Bella."

His breath calmed, and within seconds, he touched the throbbing between her legs, his forefinger moving in a circular motion with a steady heightening sense of urgency. He was still hard enough to fill her as he pushed inside her deeper and deeper. Her muscles contracted, and she followed with whispers of gratitude as her core pulsed in orgasmic release. She laid her hands on his chest to steady herself as she gathered her breaths and rolled off him but remained close to cradle in his arms in their warm, cozy bed, covered with soft luxurious linens.

"Are you all right, baby?" he asked, and she nodded, unable to speak as he kept her close in his arms. They both fell asleep, intoxicated in a post-coital haze.

Chapter Four

"Wake up. It's time to go." Miles rubbed her back, attempting to awaken her.

"What? Going where?" She tried to orient herself by looking around the room. The clock with its red numbers showed it was midnight. She stretched her nude body and looked back at her husband, who was already dressed.

"Come back to bed. I scheduled breakfast with the family from ten o'clock until noon. We'll get there when we get there." She patted his side of the bed, the sheets cool to the touch.

"We're not eating with the family this morning. We'll be in Paris."

She listened and shook her head in protest.

"Don't worry, Bella; your mother and my parents know we'll be in Paris."

"Paris? Why can't we go there later today?"

"Because, if we stay, I'll find myself at a family reunion instead of on a honeymoon, which should be for the two of us, not the entire family. Get dressed, Bella; you know I'm right."

"You're probably right." The realization of their imminent travel plans set in, and she pulled back the covers.

"The jet is already on the tarmac waiting for us, and our things will be packed and sent later today. It'll be fun and memorable. Come on. I want to share one of the most romantic cities in the world with you, as my wife." He came closer and scooped her out of the bed, depositing her at the door to the bathroom.

"Don't take too long. I'm waiting, and I'll place the outfit you had in the closet on the bed for you to slide your sexy ass into it. I assume you intended to wear it today. Move it, baby, *tout suite*." He grinned, and she looked at him, conceding there was no way she was getting out of the trip to Paris.

"What does that mean, tout—?"

"*Tout suite* is French for Pronto!"

"Oh."

She attended to her needs and took a quick shower before returning to the room to dress.

"I thought you would be a little more delighted to go to Paris." He looked at her while she searched for words to reassure him.

"I'm happy." She smiled, betraying the apprehension she had about what or who awaited them in Paris. "I thought we would spend more time in the British Isles, with the family."

"We've seen a lot of this area already. Time to move on to a new adventure." She grabbed a few of her things and placed them in her oversized handbag before he grabbed her hand and ushered her out the door.

He promised me a life of adventure. Thrills and adventure drive my man. I should be happy he wants to share them with me, but I thought he would give me more time to adjust to his desire for a ménage à trois. I should have told him I saw the sex fantasy sites he viewed on his phone of people having a threesome at various places in Paris while we were on the Fire God tour, but I thought I would have more time before he requested we try it. Don't get ahead of yourself, girl. He hasn't said anything about it, but he might.

Her shoulders hung low, and she bit her lip as she obsessed about it and worried if she was ready. She smiled, sensing he was looking at her as she prepared for their departure.

* * *

Quietly, she rode with him in the limo as he held her hand on their way to the airport. She wondered if he sensed she needed reassurance when he patted her hand. She settled into the plush leather seat in the jet for the short ride to Paris.

"This should be a smooth, quick flight. We'll be there in less than two hours."

She closed her eyes for a short nap during the flight to gather her wits and recharge her energy.

* * *

The plane hit the runway in Paris with a loud deafening thud, and the engine sounds quieted as it slowed and taxied to the terminal.

"We've arrived in the City of Lights, Paris." The captain informed them over the intercom. Bella looked out the window at the twinkling lights of the city in the distance.

"We're here, baby. A sedan is waiting for us for a brief tour of the city. Paris at night is magical."

"We've been going nonstop for the last two days, Miles. Can we find a bed and start out on a tour later today?" He cocked his head to the side after she made her request to change the plans.

"Sure, baby. Are you certain everything is all right? I didn't want to bring it up, but I know Mrs. Caspar died today and she meant a lot to you." He unbuckled his belt, and she loosened her strap to stand and stretched as he looked at her. She could tell he was concerned about how she was taking the news.

"Who told you about Mrs. Caspar?"

"One of your cousins told me to look out for you as if I had to be reminded that your concerns were now my concerns and your sadness, my sadness."

She came closer and placed her arms around him.

"I'm just tired, and no, I'm not filled with grief. I'll miss Mrs. Caspar, but I know she's at peace now, and that gives me comfort."

She was more focused on what he had planned for them in Paris and she wanted time to talk to him about his sexual proclivities later today with a clearer head.

He gave her a quick kiss and took her hand to lead her down the stairs to the tarmac, where the driver from the company he used when he toured France was waiting for them.

"Come on baby. Let's get out of here." He urged her to hurry and get in the limo before the paparazzi who regularly camped out at the airport spotted them. The driver, familiar with Miles's routine, nodded before he quickly took his seat and sped away. As they drove past the iconic sights of Paris, Bella stared wide-eyed out the window, amazed at one spectacularly illuminated site after another.

"This is amazing. I was sad we didn't get time to see more of the city while on the tour, but I knew our schedule was too tight for sightseeing." She looked at him in sheer bliss. "The pictures don't do Paris justice, and it's indescribable. Thank you for this experience." She kissed him, and with passion flowing between them, she pushed her dress off her shoulders, revealing the round mounds of her breast and flexed her back to offer them to him.

"My temptress is alert now?" He kissed the top of each breast. "I'm glad you got a little nap. You'll need all your energy for later, *mon chérie*." She sat back in her seat as he lavished her with attention.

I love him, and if a threesome is what he needs, I'll try it once for him.

She bit her nails as she looked out the window, no longer as interested in the sites of the city. The car came to a stop in front of an opulent hotel close to the avenue he pointed out was the famed Champs-Elysees. The doorman, clad in black formal attire, opened the door and welcomed them to the establishment. They bypassed the check-in desk and were escorted to the suite prepared for them before their arrival.

"If you want to resume your nap, the bedroom is right through there."

He pointed to the door carved with scrolled flourishes, fleur-de-lis, and gold leaf embellishments. She walked through the door and saw a white flowing nightgown on the bed, similar to the one the woman in the taped fantasy sex vignettes wore in the videos he'd viewed many times. Her head turned to the mixture of sounds of the doorbell, his heavy footsteps to the door across the wood floor, and to the voice of another man with a heavy French accent. Her heart fluttered, and she broke out in beads of sweat, dripping between her breast and down her back. She wrung her hands, anxious about what she imagined was about to happen.

I can do this. My marriage may depend on this. Take a little nap now and threesome later.

She paced, and unaware of the growing volume of her musings, her voice suddenly filled the room.

"I'm not ready. I don't think I can do this!" she yelled, tightening her fists at her side. Who am I kidding? I'm not some worldly sophisticate. I'm a girl from California, by way of Texas.

In an instant, she heard footsteps approaching and felt his strong arms around her. She kept her eyes low, unable to look him in the face.

"Tell me what's the matter? You've been acting strange since I told you we were coming to Paris." She heard additional footsteps coming closer to her.

"Is everything all right, Madame? I'm here for your pleasure and to ensure you have a memorable experience at my establishment." The man spoke in accented English.

Miles kept his arms around her, rubbing the goosebumps forming on her skin. She shivered, her body cool from apprehension as she looked up at the stranger in the room and gazed into the eyes of a handsome, well-dressed man.

"Bella, this is Étienne Legare, my friend and the owner of this fine establishment. He just stopped by to share his gratitude for the trip he and his wife took to Scotland on a recent holiday. They enjoyed their stay at the Middleburgh Resort, and he wanted to extend his personal congratulations on our marriage."

*Wife, marriage…*the words resonated through her head, and she calmed down. He extended his hand, caught her arm midair, and bowed. His hand slid down her forearm, and he kissed the back of her hand with his warm, soft lips.

"Pleased to meet you, Étienne."

"You're a beautiful woman, and my friend is a lucky man. My staff will take good care of the two of you during your visit to Paris. I leave you now to enjoy your time together. Let me or my manager know if you need something. Anything, my friend and it's yours." He bowed his head slightly, and Miles nodded at him as Étienne turned to leave, closing the door behind him.

He pushed the white sheer nightgown on the bed to the side and pressed her into his lap while they sat together on the bed. He caressed her hair, looked into her eyes, and spoke in soft, low tones.

"Tell me what's wrong."

"I'm not ready. I thought I could do it, but I'm not ready." He rubbed his fingers through his hair and kept her cradled in his lap.

"Ready for what? I'm confused."

"The gown on the bed is the same as the one the woman in the Paris ménage à trois videos wore. You watched those videos online so many times; I assumed you've fantasized about it. I love you, and I'll do anything to make you happy, but I'm not ready for a ménage à trois with you. I thought Étienne might be the man you wanted for our sexual… escapades. I'm glad it's not with him, but I'm still not ready for that kind of adventure."

He looked at her with a slackened jaw, wide eyes, and flared nostrils. He blinked several times before he ran his hand through his hair. She looked at him, unable to get a good read of his thoughts, so she spoke.

"Say something, anything. Are you disappointed in me?'

"Yes, I am." She covered her eyes but couldn't hold back the tears. He placed her on the bed and knelt before her.

"Please don't cry. I'm disappointed you could think I'd ever share you with another man. I love you, and I only want to be with you. I adore you Bella, and the thought of another man touching you would drive me to murderous insanity. I won't share my bed with you and another woman or another man. I have pledged myself to you and only you." She dried her tears as she listened to him.

"What about this nightgown?" She grabbed it and held it up to his face.

"Don't you recognize it? I had more soft lace placed around the collar, giving it a little more French appeal, I'll admit that, but it's yours. It's the same nightgown you wore in Texas when we made love for the first time. That night meant a lot to me, and I was just being sentimental."

She grabbed the gown and looked at the label and the sleeve, which had a slight run in the material. Then she looked up at him.

"I had your mother look through your things and send it to me. I'm glad she was cool about it and didn't ask any questions."

She laughed, imagining the telephone exchange between him and her mother, as she touched his face while she spoke.

"I love you so much, and I want to be everything you expect of a partner and a lover."

"You already are. I couldn't imagine a few years ago being married to someone as special as you. You inspire me to be the best man I can be." He turned his head and kissed her hand.

"Have you had a threesome before and do you still desire one?" She bit her lip.

"I'm a man with a past, and we need not review it. I'll just say I explored many aspects of my sexuality before I met you. So, I'll say it again, I don't want to share you with anyone else, ever."

"Good. I don't want to share you any more than I already do. I accept you have women around the world convinced they love you. You love making music, and I think I've proven I want to support your creativity because I love that part of you, but I'll not share your body with anyone, ever."

"We agree, so can we continue the honeymoon now? My knees are killing me, and I need to get up."

"Get up, silly. The honeymoon never stopped. I just wasn't sure which direction it was taking," she snickered.

He got up off his knees and stretched out with her on the bed. Then he grabbed an envelope made of fine parchment paper from under her pillow and gave it to her.

"I had this delivered to the room yesterday and had it placed under your pillow."

She sat up and turned the envelope over. A red seal embossed with a ram's head held the envelope flap tightly in place. She looked at him and hesitated before opening it.

"Go ahead, open it. I promise it's not another legal document. I wanted you to read it later after we made love, but now is as good a time as any."

"I love our synchronicity, how often we think alike. I have an envelope for you too. I'll get it and we can open our envelopes at the same time."

She left the bed and went to her handbag to retrieve the letter she'd written to him. She gave it to him, and he sniffed it, drawing pleasure from her favorite scent spritzed on the envelope.

"I wanted to watch you while you read my letter instead of reading mine at the same time." He played with her hair and shot her his puppy dog look that melted her heart every time.

"Okay, I'll read your letter first. You're not going to just stare at me while I read it, are you?"

"No, I can give you a head massage while I listen. I guess you know I enjoy playing in your hair. It makes me hot when you purr like my sex kitten."

"I don't purr."

"Yes, you do, babe, especially when I caress you with my hands in your hair."

She got up, grabbed her bamboo hairbrush out of her purse, and joined him back on the bed. She handed him the brush and nestled between his legs while he sat up, his back propped up against the many silk pillows on the bed. She traded with him, the letter he handed to her for the brush. Her head tingled under the warm touch of his fingers playing in her hair as she broke the seal of the envelope.

His voice was smooth and sexy as he spoke while she took the letter out of the envelope. "I'm glad you wanted us to exchange traditional vows, but there were still some things from my heart I wanted to share with you in private." She squirmed and tried hard to stifle a mew stuck in her throat.

Here goes. I wonder what he needed to say to me.

She unfolded the letter and began reading it. She felt the brushstrokes through her hair and the touch of his hand as he pushed her hair to the side and planted kisses along her neck while she read his thoughts line by line.

To the love of my life,
I'm imperfect in my being
but perfect in my love and commitment to you.
I pledge my fidelity to you and to place you above all others.
You are my favorite song.
Every verse I sing is about you. My chorus is:
I love you and
I'll always love you.

I promise never to leave you or forsake you.
It would cause me too much
personal pain to see your heart distressed.
God gave me a heart to love you,
eyes to see your beauty,
arms to hold you close and
A soul connected to yours.
I pledge to communicate with you as truthfully as I know how,
to protect you fiercely with all my strength,
to share my resources, including my time, treasure, and energy.

I love you,
I live for you.
I can't count the ways I feel for you because
there will never be an end to my love for you.

Loving you above all others,
forever and always,
Your husband, Miles

She finished reading the letter and held it close to her heart. He stopped brushing her hair, gently grabbed her chin, and turned her head to brush his lips against hers. Teardrops stained her letter and spoke volumes, though no words escaped her lips.

"I love you, and I'm committed to being the best husband I can be to you. I won't always get it right, but know this, Bella: I want us to be together forever. I won't let anyone come between us, and I hope you feel the same way too."

"This letter means so much to me, Miles, and I'll cherish it for the rest of my life. You couldn't have given me a more precious wedding gift. I love you so much, and I can't tell you how happy you've made me."

She leaned over to kiss him and ran her hands under his shirt, placing them on his chest close to his beating heart.

"Let's get out of these clothes. There should be more comfortable clothes in the closet for both of us, but I'd prefer if you wear the gown. I need to use the bathroom first, I'll be right back."

"Sure, I'll put on the gown, and when you get back, you can read my letter over a good glass of scotch. Do you want it neat?"

"Yes, but only a little. I've had a lot to drink over the past few days."

"Deal."

"Good." He swung his legs from around her and scooted off to the bathroom.

"Is there a sound system here? I want a little mood music!" she yelled to him.

"There's a wood cabinet in the suite's front filled with equipment and programmed music."

"A drink, music, and I will be waiting for you until you get back."

"I'll join you on the couch after I find my lounging pants." He disappeared behind the door to the bathroom while she took off all her clothes and put on the sheer, flowing white nightgown with no underwear.

She checked her reflection in the mirror and headed to the bar to fix a glass of scotch neat, and she poured a glass of Champagne from the bottle sitting in ice in a large silver bucket. After placing the drinks on the bar, she opened the cabinet in search of love songs to play while they enjoyed their early morning hours together as husband and wife. A portion of the console contained a library of music labeled in LED lights: folk music, pop, and world music. The sound of water from the shower ceased, and she heard the bathroom door open. She pressed "World Music," and a subset of the category lit up, the music of Alcazar.

"Are you familiar with a group called Alcazar?" she yelled across the suite.

"Yes, they're a popular Swedish group. Why?"

She pressed start and music came on and played throughout the suite. A slow number played, and she swayed to the music before waltzing to the open window overlooking the city.

I'm honeymooning in Paris.

She turned slowly from the window and looked in the bedroom's direction door, where Miles stood propped against the doorjamb in lounging pants tied loosely across his hips.

"Why are you staring at me?" she asked while continuing to dance.

"I'm enjoying the view."

"I agree; Paris is a beautiful city."

"Yes, she is, but you're even more enticing, and you're mine, all mine." Just as he made his way to her, the first song ended and a more upbeat number came on. She stopped in her tracks and burst out laughing as the group sang, urging the listeners to join in a ménage à trois. After she convulsed in laughter, he took her in his arms to the large plush couch where he joined in her infectious chuckling.

"I knew you wanted to do it. Let me call a few of my friends." He reached for his cell phone on the table next to the couch.

"No, don't you dare! Of all the songs to play on my honeymoon."

She continued laughing while struggling to take the phone away from him.

"I'll never share you with anyone, Miles; and two cocks coming at me would be hilarious."

They laughed so hard, she cried with glee. She caught her breath and couldn't help focusing on his hands touching her shoulder, then her breasts, filling her with feelings of passion. She returned his kisses and raised the gown over her head, tossing it on the floor, lustfully eager to join their naked bodies together.

"I hope we never lose our passion for each other."

He slid out of his pants and then laid her body on top of his. She felt his heart beating in tune with hers.

"You're the only man for me. I love the feel of you, the scent of you, and the taste of you." She slid down his body and took him into her mouth for a few delicious moments, caressing him and causing him to moan his passion. He stopped her and pulled her beneath him, kissing her soft, velvety-smooth skin, covering her breasts with reverence.

"You're my queen. I cherish you, and from tonight forward, I claim you as mine…. My lover, my wife, my life." He claimed her mouth, softly kneaded her breasts, and slid down her body to taste her engorged flesh and join with her in carnal bliss.

"Oh my gosh,, it feels so good," she declared in a loud voice.

"Shush. The security guys outside can hear you."

"I don't care. They'll be gone out of our lives soon." She writhed in delight beneath him. "I love you. I love you so much." Her body shook with joy and satisfaction.

"I don't care if the world hears me. I love you, Miles Moore." He held her tight as they lay together, struggling to catch their breaths while Latin jazz music played in the background.

"I want you to read my letter. I know it's early in the morning and now the day after our wedding, but I still think of this time as our wedding night." She lay naked on his smooth chest while he played in her hair.

"I will, baby, because I want to know what you've written to me.

We have a few more hours before daybreak, so I consider this time our extended wedding night."

She got up, put her nightgown back on, and while he was putting his pants back on, she went to the bedroom and returned, holding her letter along with the glass of scotch. She handed it to him while she sipped sparkly Champagne.

"This is good." She took another sip.

"This scotch is so smooth." He sipped from his glass and patted the cushion for her to join him on the couch. He placed the glass on the table and sniffed the scent sprayed on the envelope and took his time opening it, looking at her as he ran his finger in a slow, staccato motion under the flap until he opened it. He took the folded letter out of the envelope, and she wrapped herself in his arms as he prepared to read the musings of her heart.

I hope he feels my love in every word.

He looked at the letter and stopped reading.

"Do I have a choice of how I experience this moment?"

"I'm not sure what you're asking." She cocked her head, curious about his question.

"I'm asking you to read the letter to me. I want to hear your voice as you read your thoughts. It would make it easier for me to feel my emotions while I listen to you. I've spent so much of my life either running from my emotions or hiding them from others, and I don't want to do that with you. It would make my honeymoon present from you even more memorable if you read the letter."

She took the letter from him.

"Well, this isn't what I envisioned when I wrote it, but if it's what you want, sure I'll read it to you.' She got comfortable in his arms and read it.

"Miles, my one and only love,
I promise to love you with all my soul, my heart, and my mind.
I promise to remember that the things that endear you to me are often the same things that vex me and drive me wild. You love adventure and

novelty. You're a risk-taker, a thrill-seeker, and I promise to accept these things about you as best as I know how, even if it scares me to death.

I promise to get over it if you disappoint me and refuse my wise counsel :) because I know at some point I'll disappoint you.

I promise if you don't communicate every day with me while you're on the road working, I won't become wracked with insecurity and think you're hurt or abandoning me.

I won't try to control you or demand a guarantee from you about anything because I know life doesn't come with a warranty.

I know at the core of my being, you're the man with whom I want to share my life, the man of my wildest dreams."

Her eyes grew moist, and her breath hitched with emotions as the letter quivered a little in her shaking hand. He drew her in tight while rubbing her back. "Please continue."

She swallowed and resumed reading.

"You've given me a gift of loving the person I am, no pretenses required.

I can do me and, above all, I wish for you to continue doing you.

I've got your back, babe. I'm your ride or die chick.

I pray you continue being the wonderful man you are. Together we are imperfectly perfect for each other.

Loving you forever and a day,
Bella"

She pursed her lips tightly to hold back the flood of emotions and looked at him, hoping for a comment. She needed to hear his thoughts filling the silence in the room, something…anything, but he kept staring at her. The music had gone off after several songs, and there was no sound in the room to replace it: no laughter or voices, just the beats of silence.

Give me something.

She saw him purse his lips, and his eyes started to water. She looked at him trying to swallow hard, as if struggling to push down something, maybe his feelings, but no words, no utterings came out.

She broke the silence. "You told me you wanted to connect with your feelings. Share them with me."

"I...I've never felt so loved and understood by another person in my life. I didn't know what I was missing until I fell in love with you, and I was foolish enough to think I had everything I could want until I started wanting, loving, and needing you. Our love is precious to me, and I'll cherish it, honor it, and protect it with all my strength until I take my last breath." He held her tighter in his arms as his chest heaved, releasing the weight of his feelings. "Now that was heavy, Bella, and you've made me such a happy man."

"And you've made me a happy woman." She sealed her sentiment with a long kiss and pulled back from him, covering her mouth and the unexpected yawn.

"Excuse me, but I'm fading right now. I must accept I'll never have your stamina. Let's go to bed."

He lifted her off the couch and walked with her to the bedroom to share their bed on their first day as husband and wife.

Chapter Five

They slept until evening, and after awakening and lounging around their suite, he promised they would spend additional time in Paris so he could show her the magic of the city in daylight.

They were granted special permission to tour the Louvre together the following day before it opened to the public: Étienne's wedding gift to them.

"I know it's too much to ask, but I wish our honeymoon could go on forever, just the two of us." She swung her hand in his as they toured the galleries.

"I can't promise you that, but I'll give you all of me now. Our life back in California will be a change for both of us, but I think we're up to the challenges."

"I agree. We should just enjoy being in this blissful moment for now with no intrusive thoughts of the future." She walked with him, enjoying the art treasures of Paris, briefly biting her lip as if to bind her uncertainty.

I pray I'm up to the challenge.

She shrugged off the anxious thought and tightened her grip, which he rewarded with a kiss as he hugged her shoulders.

After the second day, they left Paris and traveled on a whim back to Rome on a detour to their destination: Venice. They had been too busy preparing for the concert when they'd been in Rome weeks ago to visit any of the sites.

"Where are we going?" She stepped out of the limo early in the morning and grabbed his hand as they walked down sunny, narrow cobblestone streets.

"Follow me. I'll tell you about it when we get there."

"A man of surprises." She smiled at him, and he flashed her a bright, gorgeous smile, causing her insides to quiver with giggly excitement. In the past, she didn't like surprises or being led to a location unfamiliar to her, but she took his hand anyway, disarmed by his handsome face and eagerness to share his delights.

She once needed to feel in control to keep her nerves in check, but since giving herself heart and soul to him, something had changed inside her. Her universe had shifted and was revolving on a different axis. She no longer felt life was something that came at you and you had to be prepared to deal with it. She was more open to new experiences; they were now a source of excitement rather than something to dread.

The narrow streets they passed were lined with many cafes and restaurants. Women walked by with small children in tow, seemingly inattentive to the sounds of gushing water growing in a crescendo of sound, and then, as if a magical gift was given to them from the gods, they turned the corner and suddenly the gorgeous sight of Trevi Square with the ornate fountain glistening in the sun stood in front of them. She stopped, but he pulled her forward.

"This is breathtaking." She took in a breath and tried to grab for her phone.

"This is the famous Trevi Square and before us the Trevi fountain."

"Wait, I want to take a picture."

"Can we live in the moment? I promise we can take as many pictures as you want later. Come on." A few people had already gathered in front of the fountain despite the early time of day.

She strolled toward the imposing carved figures made of old

travertine stone.

"My uncle brought me and NeNe here as children to share his love of architecture with us. The statues are examples of Baroque architecture, and the central figure is Neptune, God of the Sea. There's a legend associated with throwing three coins into the fountain, and I'm changing the meaning behind it, but we shouldn't forget to place our right hand over our left shoulder and toss the coins."

He pulled out three coins from his pocket and gave them to her. She turned her back to the fountain as he had done.

"The first coin is to ensure we return to Rome." They threw the first coin into the huge fountain, with carved horses, oversized figurines, and sprays of water arching from various nozzles, creating bubbles throughout the stone pool.

"This one signifies my hope that our love grows stronger every day." They tossed their second coin.

"The last one," he pressed the coin between his fingers, "signifies a blessing for a long and happy marriage."

They threw their final coin together and kissed. They had on sunglasses and ball caps as disguises, but glancing over his shoulder; he saw members of the paparazzi had noticed them and were getting closer.

"We'd better go." He grabbed her hand and ushered her away quickly.

"Why do we have to go?"

"I'll explain it to you in the car." He hurried her back through the narrow streets and into the back seat of the limo waiting for them. The driver sped away as the crowds gathering in the streets around the fountain hampered the paparazzi from getting any closer.

"I'm trying to protect our privacy as much as I can, and I don't want to share our honeymoon with the paparazzi." She looked as he tapped his foot, then crossed and uncrossed his leg.

"I appreciate your efforts, and I wondered why so many tourist sites we visited prior to today had so few people around, but I figured you had something to do with it, especially when the restaurants had only a few or no other patrons. Thank you for shielding our time from the paparazzi, but I don't want you to think this is my expectation of our lives together in California. I'll still be the chief marketing officer at AriMusic. I know what comes with the territory."

"You plan to continue in your position?" He sat up, his back stiff and erect.

"Yes." She was unwavering in her response.

"I just thought—I'll adjust to you continuing in your current position. No need to discuss business on our honeymoon." He smiled and settled back in his seat.

"I have another surprise for you, Bella."

"What great adventure have you planned now?" She took a breath, relieved they wouldn't mar their honeymoon with talk of business.

"We're going to the luxury terminal to board a train with a private car to view the scenic Italian countryside between Rome and Venice. I loved this trip when I took it years ago to unwind after a tour."

She snuggled into his arms. "You're full of surprises—and all of them good. Thanks for our trip back to Rome. I've heard a lot about Venice, and I can't wait to ride in a gondola with you," she said, tingling with delight.

"Touring Europe is much better with you and without the stress of performing in concert." He grabbed her hand and planted a kiss on top of it.

* * *

They boarded the train, and he slept while she snapped pictures as the train slowed and traveled to different stations along the countryside, dotted with quaint farmhouses, low-growing grasses, tall cypress trees, and olive trees.

They finally arrived in Venice and stayed in a villa over the water, spending two weeks eating, sightseeing, and making love. Traversing the area along the Grand Canal, they meandered through the narrow streets of the city, marveling at the architecture and cathedrals and enjoying the delicious smells wafting from the many restaurants dotted along their course.

The gondola ride was one of the high points. Their gondolier, dressed in a striped navy tee shirt and straw boat hat with a matching band, rowed the boat gracefully through the canals with his toned arms and muscular hands firmly on long oars. Miles joined him in serenading her during their ride.

"That was fantastic, and I loved your serenade. Did you also arrange for the women waiting on the dock to accompany you in song?" she asked back at the villa.

"No, I just sang a popular song. I knew someone would join in."

A month went by as they crisscrossed throughout Italy together. The paparazzi finally caught up with them in Florence. They laughed at the magazine photo of them viewing Michelangelo's marble statue of a male nude representing the biblical David. The picture had a quote from Bella she wasn't aware someone had overheard.

"He's got nothing on you, baby," someone quoted her. The photo showed him looking at her sheepishly, but his chest was puffed out as she pointed at the naked statue.

"I'd better watch my tongue. This month away has made me forget there's always a hot mic around," she snickered.

"A hot mic doesn't matter if you're speaking the truth of my stuff. Who would know better than you?"

She gave him a quick side-eyed glance and thought it best not to answer.

They woke up late the next morning after a night of dancing and wine tasting to enjoy a nice breakfast and leisure time together. Neither one of them wanted to mention that time was drawing near and the honeymoon was ending soon.

"Things will be hectic when we return home. Are you sure you don't mind if I return to Scotland to do a concert?" He finished his last bite of food.

"We've had a month together, and I think it's a good idea for you to perform for your fans in Scotland while I move into the estate."

She finished her breakfast, which had been prepared for them by the villa's staff and placed on the piazza. She got up out of her seat and used her crooked index finger to motion to him to follow her back to the bedroom.

"Great lovemaking should always follow a great breakfast, and I'm hungry for my husband."

" I'm pleased to comply with my wife's wishes." He wiped his mouth with his napkin and got up to return with her to the bedroom.

* * *

The Fire God tour was a financial success despite the cancellation of some of the dates. After their honeymoon, she left to visit her mother in Texas and then returned to California to supervise the move to her new home. The newlyweds kept in touch often, calling each other multiple times a day while Miles remained in Europe to headline an intimate gathering of VIP guests at the Middleburgh Resort.

The show was a scaled-down version of his usual performance, but they taped it for viewing by a larger audience later in the year. Bella came up with the marketing ideas, and Parker completed the plan for video merchandising of the concert. He promised her during one of their many phone calls that he would be home in a little more than a week.

Bella used her bonus check from the Fire God tour to refurbish her father's bike. After taking delivery of it earlier in the week, she couldn't wait until Miles got home to take it out for a long ride. Only a week had passed since she'd last seen him, but she missed him terribly. The last time they'd communicated, he couldn't commit to coming home sooner than expected, and she hadn't told him about her new bike. She had a few surprises too.

She twitched with excitement, looking at her new bike every day, and she couldn't convince herself to put it off any longer. Although she hadn't ridden by herself in years, she planned to take a ride along the canyon. She woke up early the next morning, put on her clothes, and grabbed a breakfast bar before running to her bike.

Every woman deserves her secrets, she told herself. She left before Mr. Curtis, their estate manager, and most of the housekeeping crew arrived at work.

***

Hours later, Miles arrived home to surprise her. With flowers in hand, he yelled for her to come downstairs.

"I have a surprise for you, Bella." He yelled out as he entered the door.

He planned to teach her how to ride a motorcycle so they could enjoy relaxing rides together. The ride on his Ecosse had been the beginning of their romantic relationship and had brought her such joy, so he'd had two new custom-made Harleys delivered to the house. She didn't answer him, so he went back outside when Mr. Curtis came out to help with his bags and to welcome him home.

"I had the garage manager pull out the bikes hidden in the garage and park them in the driveway."

"Thanks, Mr. Curtis; where's Bella?"

"The missus isn't home. I haven't seen her all morning." Mr. Curtis took the bags to their private suite while he searched the house to confirm her absence. Miles called her on her cell, but she didn't answer. He checked with Darien, his executive assistant, and Reagan, and they hadn't heard from her. He decided against calling her mother since he didn't want to cause alarm and instead chose to stay calm by telling himself she would be home soon. He tried calling her again, but still she still didn't answer. He played with Bosco, his beloved dog, who seemed to sense his master's worry.

Patience was never his virtue and he went to the garage to check.

"All the cars are in place," he assured himself.

His worry intensified with time, and he blamed himself for decreasing the security detail assigned to his new wife after her return home. He thought she would be safely back in the States behind the gates of the estate—and the death threats he received as a celebrity were directed at him, never at her.

I hope I haven't made a fatal mistake.

His pulse quickened and he paced back and forth, trying to decide what to do next. He rubbed his chest as his heart pounded from fear.

"Enough of this shit."

He pulled out his phone and called Bradley, his head of security.

"Bradley, I'm reversing my decision. Activate a security group and find my wife now. Bella is missing."

"Alright, but didn't you tell me to pull back on the group assigned to Bella? And what do you mean she's missing?"

"No one knows where she is, so now I'm telling you to alert every man we got to find her and I'll deal with her anger later."

"Will do, and I'll get back to you as soon as I have some answers."

After hanging up, he went outside to his archery set, picked up his bow, and landed one sharpened arrow after another in the bullseye in hopes of discharging some of his pent-up fear and anger. He threw the bow to the ground and made tight fists alongside his body, frustrated his attempts to distract himself weren't working.

Turning to the sound of an engine approaching, he saw a sleek black sports car coming up the driveway, which parked before reaching the front of his home. He didn't recognize the car, but he walked toward the vehicle and saw Corey Baker get out and go to the passenger side to open the door for a woman with long legs and waist-length, straight black hair. She had bronze skin, denoting probable mixed heritage, and the brown eyes of a goddess. He looked at Corey, stopped, and threw his head back.

"Great. Bella is missing, her ex is in my driveway, and now I have to deal with him, " he bristled.

Corey placed his hand in the small of the woman's back and, with a relaxed posture, sauntered toward him. He cast his eyes on the woman and gazed at Miles as he walked with pride toward him.

Miles recognized the woman as Nadia Eastman, one of his many former companions. The roar of a bike broke their attention as a rider dressed in black attire on a Harley came up the hill and stopped between the two parties approaching each other.

He strained his vision to see the rider, who looked like Bella, and sighed with relief as she cut the motor to the bike after coming to an abrupt stop.

Taking her time, she got off the bike and took off her helmet. Miles widened his stance and opened and then shut his mouth as he fisted his hands at his sides, his fears lessened now that she had returned from her long ride. He looked at her as she ran her hand through her hair and shook her head to release excess moisture out of her hair. Bella smiled at him as she removed her jacket to reveal her wet black t-shirt, which clung tightly to her chest and was tucked into her leather pants, which hugged her hips and legs in the right places. Miles relaxed his posture but remained tight-lipped with his arms folded across his chest.

He saw Nadia nudge Corey, trying to sway his attention away from Bella, who was running full speed toward Miles. Miles unfolded his arms just in time to catch her as she leaped into his embrace and placed her hands alongside his face to direct her tongue into his mouth. He took her in his arms and returned the kiss.

"Why didn't you tell me you were coming home early?"

"I wanted to surprise you with a gift of two custom Harleys." He pointed to the his and hers bikes behind him. "I thought I would teach you to ride, but I see it's not necessary."

She leaned into him. "I'm sure there are lots of things you can teach me."

He watched as she turned to face Corey and Nadia.

"I'm surprised to see you, Corey. It's been a while since we last saw each other. What brings you here today?"

He handed her a leather-bound folder.

"I thought I should return these papers to you. They are plans for projects with some of your other clients. You left them at my place almost a year ago."

He looked at Nadia. "Excuse my manners. Let me introduce my girlfriend, Nadia Eastman. Nadia, this is Ari Moore and Bella Wahlberg."

Bella extended her hand to Nadia, and Miles nodded but didn't extend his hand. She looked at him and he raised an eyebrow.

"Her name is Bella Moore, Corey. I'm sure you heard we got married last month."

"Yes, I did. I found it interesting you got married so soon, since

Bella always spoke of establishing her career before getting married and having children. Are the two of you expecting?" He asked while keeping his arm around Nadia, who shifted her weight under his arm.

Bella responded, decreasing the awkward tension that was quickly developing.

"Corey, you shouldn't have troubled yourself to come this far out of your way, but I appreciate your thoughtfulness. Miles is back in town after a long tour, so please excuse us. I need to give my husband the welcome home he deserves. Thanks again and goodbye."

She turned to leave, and Miles took her by the hand as they walked up the driveway, leaving Corey and Nadia behind. Now that he knew Bella was safe and in his arms, Miles felt his taut shoulder muscles relax, and he stopped to show her the new bikes before going inside their home. Kissing and playing with each other blissfully as they reunited, they didn't notice Corey and Nadia driving away.

Once inside the house, he leaned her against the wall as he lifted her legs and she wrapped them around him.

"You know Nadia, don't you?"

"The answer is yes, and I don't want to talk about her. He only brought her here to impress you, anyway." He kissed her in between laughs at Corey's expense. "I want you now. We'll talk about them later. You're hot as hell in that outfit."

He grabbed her and tossed her over his shoulder, taking the stairs to the bedroom two at a time. She hung over his shoulder and swatted him on the butt.

"Yeah, baby, keep turning me on. You know how to welcome a man back home."

He locked the door to their suite of rooms and tore off his clothes to reveal a raging hard-on.

"Let me shower and change first." She tried to get to the bathroom.

"Don't worry, baby. You'll be drenched in sweat when I finish with you."

He pressed a few buttons and the privacy panels on the windows descended.

She took off her clothes and shivered from the chill in the room.

"Come here, babe, and let me warm you up." He beckoned her to him and they kissed, enjoying the fiery passion as their bodies physically connected with each other, reigniting desires that had smoldered during their time apart. His chest heaved as he settled between her legs, and they joined together as one. She rolled her hips, and he fell into her dark eyes, dilated from the burning heat set ablaze by their reunion. He hungered for her touch and was surprised that only a week away from her felt like an eternity.

"No one can ever compete with you for my love. I'm yours."

"Yes, you're mine," he reminded her and took her over the brink to ecstasy.

They didn't have a care in the world. Bella had returned home and she was safe in his arms.

Chapter Six

It delighted Bella that Miles took an additional six weeks instead of a month off from studio work and touring. They spent a whirlwind month in Charlotte, North Carolina, with his extended family members for celebrations with his maternal relatives of Hispanic descent, the Tavares family, and with his multi-cultural paternal relatives, the Moores. She loved spending most of their time with the energetic, high-achieving Moore family. She and NeNe became closer as they spent time together while Miles hung out with his male relatives. She was grateful for the chance to realize her dream of fun with a large family and to experience Christmas in New York for the first time.

"Miles, the walk down Fifth Avenue yesterday with the wonderful holiday-themed store windows was fantastic. Mom, Reagan, and Darien will love the presents I bought for them. I think I enjoyed visiting the toy stores more than Parker's kids will enjoy the toys I purchased for them."

Her smile faded as she looked at the pictures she'd uploaded to her laptop. His parents and twin sisters, Anne-Marie and Allison, were out for the day, and they were alone in the brownstone.

He looked at her. "You look a little sad."

She lowered the lid of her laptop and addressed him as he sat across the table from her, enjoying a beer.

"I loved spending time with your sisters yesterday. They wanted to take me on a special tour of their New York, and then we were to meet your mother and NeNe for lunch at an outdoor bistro. 'Wear something casual and make sure you have on comfortable shoes,' they told me. I woke up, and it was unusual you were still in bed, so I grabbed something casual out of my suitcase and kept the lights low so I wouldn't wake you after your long jam session with your father."

He yawned and took another sip of his beer.

"Am I boring you?" She frowned.

"No, I'm listening, go ahead with your story."

"Well, I put on my white polo shirt trimmed in gold and yellow with the small emblem of the Golden Gate Bridge, blue jeans, and my white Chucks. I had my hair up and put on just a little makeup. I was ready for the day, and I went to the kitchen to grab a power drink before we began our adventure. The girls were in the kitchen, and they're both twin teen chic. They could have posed for the cover of any fashion magazine, and I thought I should change, but they told me I looked fine. We had a great time in and out of several boutiques, and then we headed to the restaurant where NeNe and your mother, both dressed in business attire, joined us after a meeting for your family's charity, and here I was underdressed for the occasion. No one said anything though, not even outspoken NeNe. The food was fantastic, and we were about to go the car when the paparazzi came and shot pictures of us, including me, plain Jane."

"My family is used to having their pictures taken around town. You know my father is a famous jazz player even by New York's standards, and you probably won't be tagged in the photos. Relax, it's no big deal."

"Really? Just like it's no big deal when I fell at Rockefeller Center while we were ice skating?"

"No, but it was funny. The kid fell in front of you, you panicked and fell on your ass. I told you to skate with me, but no, Ms. Independent had to skate by herself."

"If it was no big deal, why are these photos on several sites with the caption, 'Bella Moore choking on her bite of the Big Apple'?" She raised the lid and turned her laptop so he could scroll through the pictures.

"You know how these things go. You're in the news today, and someone else will be in the news tomorrow."

She sighed and continued to lament.

"I'm used to crafting the news and determining which pictures will be featured in my job as a marketing professional—I don't want to be the news story."

"It comes with the territory of being married to a celebrity. My mother said it took her some time to adjust too, but you'll get used to it." He took her hand and led her to the family room near the kitchen, then closed the door behind them. He led her to the couch, but she took a seat in the chair nearest to him.

"You're my wife, and you're now part of the news connected to me. I know you want to continue in your role at the company, but you can't be the workhorse and the show pony at the same time. We'll have lots of media appearances, and you'll need time to prepare to be in front of the camera. There's not enough time in the day to arrange the appearances and be a subject of the event at the same time."

"I plan to keep my appearances to a minimum. I'm not the star—you are. Give me a chance to see if I can make it work. If not, we can go back to being friends," she said, playing with him.

"Hell no! You'll give up your job and stand by my side as my wife."

"I don't plan to be a prop, standing silently while journalists interview you. I'll always attend the major events, but I'll not be an ever-present but silent part of the story. I've worked too hard to give up my career."

"All right. We'll see how it works out. I don't think my family is coming home until later this evening. Why don't you and I take advantage of this time together? You've had so much girl time with my family, I've gotten a little lost in the shuffle. I miss you, and I need your attention." He arched his back and raised his hips off the couch to lower his jeans and underwear to his knees.

"Come to me."

"Right here and now? In your parents' house? What if we get caught?"

"They aren't coming back soon. I think my father told me they planned to eat at my uncle's house while we enjoy a little private time."

"We'd better not get caught." She moved over to the couch, and he lifted her on top of him. She had on a short dress, and he raised her hem, revealing her thong.

"I'm getting used to my girl from Texas riding me." She lowered herself onto him and gyrated her hips as the thought of discovery heightened the tensions between them.

"That's right, baby. Have your way with me."

She lowered the zipper in front of her dress and revealed her breasts moving up and down in her red laced demi-cup bra.

"Jingle bells, jingle bells. Oh, what fun it is to romp with Bella in the hay, yeah!" he sang, slowly pumping into her. She swatted his arm and held his hips, moving up and down to the cadence of his voice. She felt her core tightening as the pace of his thrusting increased. Her head turned toward the door with the unexpected sound of footsteps in the front of the house.

"Stay with me, baby. Focus. We're almost there." He thrusted one more time and pulled her head to his to seal her mouth and muffle her scream.

"Miles, Bella? Is everything all right?" The sound of Lecia's voice suspended the action.

"Yeah, Mami. Give us a minute. We'll be right out!" he yelled to her.

His father Cade called out to them in a loud voice, "Hey Miles and Bella. We're back earlier than we planned. We'll be in the front room, so don't rush. Come out when you're ready."

"I told you we'd get caught!" She rolled off him and tried to catch her breath and straighten her dress at the same time.

"You know it was good, and we didn't get caught. They interrupted us," he corrected while pulling up his underwear and closing the front of his pants.

She straightened her hair and tried to smooth the wrinkles out of her dress.

"You look fine." He extended his hand and escorted her to the front of the house.

She felt the heat crawl up her neck and face as she faced his parents and twin sisters.

"Hi, Bella and Miles," his sisters greeted them before returning their attention back to their phones.

"If you'll excuse us, we have homework to finish," Allie was the usual spokesman for the two.

"Right. The two of you are off to do homework on your holiday break?" Lecia repositioned the shopping bags in her hand.

"Yes, Mami," they both chimed in and ran off to their room.

"I hope the two of you enjoyed your time together. I know the girls have craved attention from both of you, and they don't understand a newlywed's need for privacy. It's just the girls were young when you left, Miles, and they're thrilled to have the time to reconnect with you and to get to know Bella. Oh, these things are for you, Bella. I hope you like them." She handed several bags to her and encouraged her to open them.

Bella went to the couch and opened the bags, filled with casual outfits, formal gowns, and shoes.

"You shouldn't have, Lecia. These clothes are gorgeous. Thank you—you're so thoughtful."

Miles looked at her, smiling as she opened the presents.

"Mami, Bella has closets full of things in California. She purchased more things in Europe and I bought her things. We appreciate your generosity, but you need not worry. Pops has taught me the benefits of lavishing gifts on the women we love."

Lecia refused to be deterred and shook her head.

"Well, Bella can leave some things here for events when the two of you come back. We're always out and around town, and she can't be expected to pack things for all occasions. People are judgmental, and some of my friends—no, my associates—contacted me to ask what beef I had with Bella. They told me they saw pictures on social media, and we shouldn't have embarrassed her by failing to remind her she was in New York, not laid-back California. They can talk about me, but I'll not have them make fun of Bella, and I told them so. I'll not have anyone making fun of any of my children." She narrowed her eyes and tightened her lips. Bella looked at Miles and then his parents as all of them stood without commenting on Lecia's concerns for a few seconds.

"Anybody want a beer?" Cade broke the heavy silence.

"No, thank you," they all answered.

His father motioned for Miles to join him in another room, and they left the women alone to finish the discussion.

"I'm sorry I embarrassed you. I guess casual means something different to me than to some women in New York." Bella looked at Lecia with sad eyes.

"You didn't embarrass me." Lecia went to the couch to help Bella gather the wrappings from the presents.

"If I was angry with anyone, it would be with myself. I've been in your position, and I know what it's like to have someone measure everything about you: how you fix your hair, the makeup you wear, your weight, your facial expressions, what you say, and how you act. The scrutiny can overwhelm anyone, and I want nothing to cause friction between the two of you. You've been a bridge between me and my son, and I want to make sure you know how thankful I am to you."

Bella leaned over and hugged her.

"Thank you for welcoming me into the family with open arms. People scrutinized me for not having the right outfits and for not fitting into the right social circles when I was a teenager. I think that's why I was comfortable not being in the limelight and keeping the focus on Miles, but I can handle it."

"Good, and please know I'm available when you need to kvetch."

"Thanks, Lecia. I'll probably need your support in the months to come."

* * *

They returned to California in the new year on their luxury private jet. Bella had had so much wine during the six weeks of brunches, dinner gatherings, and family meet and greets that she turned down the offer for alcohol on their enjoyable flight home. The steward provided Miles with a drink while she retired to their bedroom.

She went through her overnight bag and found her moisturizer for her face and the body lotion Lecia had given her, with instructions to use it before bed, but she had difficulty locating her birth control pills. She applied the lotion and went through her bag again in search of her pills and still couldn't find them. Placing a hand on her chest, she tried to slow the rhythm of her heart, which was pounding as droplets of sweat broke out over her brow.

I wonder where I could have placed them.

They had attended a surprise goodbye party thrown in their honor last night, which had left them little time to pack. There were so many private flights leaving out of New York that they couldn't change the departure time without risking a delay or being rerouted to land in an airport farther away from their home. Their pilot had already filed their flight plans and cautioned them not to change it at the last minute. She searched her bag, turning the contents upside down on her lap, but since she still couldn't find the missing pills, she finally accepted she'd left her birth control pills at his parents' home in New York.

Distracted by increasing anxiety as she searched frantically through her bag, she didn't notice Miles staring at her until she turned and looked up into his caring brown eyes. She was thankful he'd shared his family with her and given her the time to get to know them better, but she knew he would not be pleased she had misplaced her pills…again.

Shit. Calm down, you can handle this. She took in a deep breath. Maybe it's providential that I can't find my pills. I can't think of a greater gift than sharing a child with him. She sighed, her attempts to soothe herself failing. I fucked up…nice choice of words, girl. Fucked up and maybe knocked up.

"You know I'm not shooting blanks, so don't get mad at me if you end up pregnant," he'd warned during their time in Italy. Despite his concerns earlier, she still couldn't get it together in taking her pills at the same time each day. She had complained about the jet lag and fatigue, but really, she had no excuse.

"I think I left my pills on the nightstand in New York." She waited for another admonishment from him, but instead, he walked toward her in silence until he reached the bed and sat down.

"Ah, hmm." He yawned and looked at her with heavy-lidded eyes.

"Let's get some rest. We have several hours left before we land in Los Angeles. Baby, I need some sleep."

She slipped under the covers with him, surprised he wasn't angry with her nor concerned she had forgotten to take her pill.

He was tired, but it didn't stop him from moving closer and pressing against her.

"You smell so good. What's that scent you're wearing? It's so sensual."

"Your mother gave me some lotion to wear at night. Do you like it?"

"Oh, yes. It turns me on."

He looked into her eyes and sank his tongue deep into her mouth, causing her to lean her head back to take in all of him. He licked along her lower lips and pulled her legs up around him.

"I will make sweet memories with you, girl. Welcome to the mile-high club," he told her as he pulled her panties to the side and sank into her heat. The heightened passion between them, and the turbulence in the air, added to the mounting excitement. It was hard for her to be white- knuckled with fear in a shaking plane when he had her hot with passion. They spooned with each other and reflected briefly on their personal growth after they finished their lovemaking.

"I'm the best version of me when I'm with you. I'm strong and fearless." She rested in his arms, sated with pleasure.

"Your willingness to be vulnerable is your strength, Bella. You're loving and so accepting of others. You see people's needs instead of wasting time examining their shortcomings. I can take off the mask that fame requires me to wear when I'm with you."

She turned and looked into his eyes.

"I love you and I don't need all the trappings of success. I'll always love the stripped-down version of you better than the Ari persona with the toys, the money, and the fame."

"I know that, and I'm a lucky man to have you as my wife."

They were both tired and fell asleep for a nap together.

His hand stroking her hair and his lips taking in her breasts woke her moments later.

"Can I entice you to do something with me?"

"Let me guess? You want to play some…oh, so good…play some more?" His fingers played between her legs, causing her to experience a loss for words as he kissed the angle of her chin, then down the side of her neck.

"Yes, play with me." He entered her and slowly rolled his hips, touching all her hot spots.

"What…oh my gosh…do you want me to do?"

"Move with me." He grabbed her legs and wrapped them around his hips, increasing the friction between them as he plunged his tongue into her mouth and sunk deep within her at the same time the plane dropped suddenly in altitude. His thrusts came at a frenzied pace as the jet leveled off before taking a steep upward angle back to a higher altitude.

"I'm going to scream!" She yelled out her orgasm as he took them both over the edge.

"Did you tell the pilot to do acrobatics with the plane?" She caught her breath and hit him on the chest.

"If you liked it, then yes I did. Don't worry, we were safe. Our pilot is a former military officer. He loves doing evasive maneuvers. You said you loved the thrill-seeker in me."

"I also said you vex me too." She settled in his arms. "No more surprises. I want to get to California in one piece." She yawned and fell back asleep.

* * *

"Ten minutes before we land in Los Angeles," the captain announced. "There's a little turbulence, so please return to your seats and buckle up."

They scurried back to their seats and buckled their belts.

"Never order the pilot to do maneuvers again," she reminded him.

"All right, I won't, but tell me one thing, did you enjoy the sex last night?"

"You know I did. My orgasm was one of the best I've ever had." He looked over at her and stared.

"Who gave you the best one?" He frowned and waited for her answer.

"You did, the first time you made love to me."

He beamed, her answer changing his countenance as he moved his shoulders and chest, puffed up with pride.

"You really know how to wrap me around your fingers Bella. Don't think I'm not aware of the power you have over me."

"I don't need power over you Miles, and I never want to feel like I'm controlling you. Just knowing we love each other and are willing to make sacrifices to keep our marriage strong is enough.

"I hear you, and I can't promise that when I'm afraid, it won't feel like I'm being controlling, but I promise I'll back off when you remind me I'm crossing the line."

She smiled at him and reached out for his hand.

"We got this baby, as long as we stay true to our vows and communicate our feelings. Nothing is off limits, and nothing is off the table when it comes to telling each other the truth."

"Agreed." He reached over to kiss her.

"Deal." She smiled back at him

They felt the wheels descend before the plane hit the runway and taxied into the terminal.

He took out his cell, set on airplane mode for safety during the flight, and when he resumed regular mode, his cell immediately blew up with messages, including a missed call from Parker, his CFO at AriMusic.

He returned his call, and she looked at him, knowing the vacation was over.

"Miles, Darien and Bradley are here with me. I have great news for you, bro. Your nominations for the music awards include Hip-hop Male Performer of the Year, Best Album of the Year, and Song of the Year. Get your ass off the plane so I can call a press conference for you. You did it, man. Miles, you're at the top. Where's Bella?"

"She's beside me, but we'll need some time to prepare before I go before the press. We've had a long flight, and we need to freshen up. I'll talk to you when we get home."

She gathered her things as he told her the good news.

"That's wonderful, babe; another press conference." She smiled brightly, hoping it hid her disappointment. She'd had hopes of spending a quiet night together, but she knew her obligations, and duty called. They disembarked and hurried to a black limousine waiting on the tarmac. She got in and snuggled close to him on the ride home.

* * *

They had just enough time to shower and change clothes. She ran to the bathroom, fumbling to get a pill out her back-up birth control pill dispenser.

"Bella, hurry. I want you with me at the press conference tonight. We're going to be late," he yelled to her through a partially closed door. "Come on, babe."

"*Estoy llegando, Papi,*" she yelled back to him. Since spending time with his family, they had incorporated Spanglish into their conversations.

He pushed the door open and accidentally bumped into her.

Damn! She frowned at the dispenser, now floating in the toilet.

"*Que dice*, Bella?"

"I said, I'm coming. You made me drop my pills." She looked into the toilet at the destroyed pills.

"Si, vendras, mi amor." *Yes, you will come, my love*, he teased. He grabbed her around the waist and pushed her up against the wall, unfazed her pills were destroyed as he planted kisses along her neck. She purred with pleasure as the heat of his breath against her skin sent tingles down her spine.

"Tomame ahora, Papi." She looked into his eyes, skin flushed and chest heaving.

"I'll gladly take you now." He had difficulty containing his lust, but she urged him to respond to the phone ringing in his pocket while she held on with her hands around his neck and her legs wrapped around his waist.

"It's Parker again." He frowned at the face on the screen and answered it.

"Parker, handle the press conference and take Darien with you. Bella isn't feeling up to going out, and I need to stay with her for tonight. Bye."

He hung up the phone, and as he looked into her eyes, she smiled, imagining all the things he would do to her.

"Take me, baby. I'm all yours," she told him and he smiled, walking with her in his arms to the bedroom.

Chapter Seven

Elated by the news, Miles told Bella that his father, Cade, was the recipient of the Lifetime Achievement Award for Excellence in Jazz, and his mentor, Jay Truth, was the recipient of the Legend in Hip-hop Award. NeNe and Parker were busy negotiating the terms of an agreement for him to perform his music and take part in the tribute to Jay at the music awards show. Bella knew he believed in bringing his best to the stage, so she accepted that Miles, his band along with the dancers, including Reagan Madison, would be practicing at their home studio every day.

She and Reagan had become even closer since the tour's performance in Scotland, and sometimes, Bella worked out with the dancers to stay in shape, but she knew she would never be as good as the professionals or asked to be a substitute, even though she knew the routines.

Six weeks had passed since they'd returned from New York, and it was good basking in the California sun instead of living through one of the East Coast's winters in January and February. She was happy they left the Big Apple right after the holidays.

Today, she relaxed in the pool instead of dancing. She enjoyed the time floating on the Ledge Lounger while the dancers worked out a routine poolside instead of in the rehearsal room. Miles was somewhere in the house, going over the music with the band while the staff brought a light lunch out to the patio for everyone to enjoy.

"I don't know what it is, but you're glowing today. Your skin is so bright, and your hair is getting thicker. Do you have a new glam squad?" Reagan asked.

"No, I do my own beauty routine, if you want to call it a beauty routine. Come join me in the pool. You deserve some time to relax." She pointed to the pool house. "There are lots of bathing suits in there. I'm sure one of them fits you."

Before long, Reagan and the other dancers were in bathing suits frolicking in the pool. Someone turned on the music, and a poolside dance party began. Bella got out of the pool and joined in the dance party, wearing a black two-piece bikini.

She felt Miles's presence, looked up, and saw him as he stared at her, enjoying her dance with the girls. She turned for a fuller view of him standing above them on the balcony and his focus on her, intense, like a laser, made her feel as if they were experiencing an unshared private moment while her awareness of the dancers faded into the background. He remained eerily quiet for seconds before saying anything.

"Bella, baby, can I see you upstairs? For the rest of you, the party is over, time to get back to work." He didn't comment further at the dancers' low grumble of protest.

"Sure, Miles. I'll be right there." Bella placed her hand over her brow to shield her eyes from the sun.

"Mister Miles wants us to get back to work," Reagan whispered to Bella, aware Miles was still looking at them.

He backed away from the balcony, never breaking eye contact with her until he crossed the threshold to their bedroom. She'd slipped on a light cover-up before going up to their suite.

Before she'd met him, she couldn't see herself dancing in a bikini, not even at home. They had affected each other in ways she hadn't thought were possible. She was more relaxed and comfortable in her skin, and he wasn't as obsessed with perfection. This was the day before the award show, and he wasn't barking orders at the band as he had before the start of the Fire God tour.

She reached the suite and shut the door behind her. He was facing the window with his back to her.

"You looked gorgeous out there, dancing as if you didn't have a care in the world."

She blushed in response to his unexpected compliment. "I'm sure that's not what you wanted to tell me. What's up?"

"Right. My mind went blank for a moment looking at your luscious body. Darien told me you gave surrogate permission to change the name of a song I dropped yesterday on the airwaves. I named the song 'Bella' and you changed the title to 'You.' Is that true?"

She walked lightly toward him and laid her hands on his back.

"Yes, I did. I thought the title 'You' had more of a universal appeal. Studies have shown heartthrobs shouldn't name songs after their love interests. Female fans like it when they can fantasize about their idols."

He didn't answer her, a sign she knew meant he was unhappy, but he drew her arms closer around his waist. She leaned against his back as he continued to look out the window.

"You're not my love interest. You're my wife, and I don't care about studies or polls. I love you, and I want the world to know how you changed my life for the better. You're the goddess of my fire, my Pele."

She stroked his back with a tender touch. "Don't be mad at me. I love you, and I don't want to hurt your career. I see posts like: '*Ari is limp and soft in love*,' and, '*Bella has whipped the fire out of Ari*.' Even with the change in the title, the song hasn't climbed the charts as fast as your other songs." She turned to rest her face on his back. "I'm sorry if I upset you."

"I'm not angry with you. I'm confused, that's all. Why would you want to remain in the shadows when you've contributed so much to our recent success? We're a team, aren't we? At least, that's how I see it."

He turned and took her in his arms.

"Don't worry about me. You need to focus on the show tomorrow. I know it means a lot to you and to me too. We can talk about teamwork later." She changed the subject to lighten up the mood. "I'm excited to see your family again. What time are they arriving?"

"*Our* family, Bella, and they won't be in until hours before the show tomorrow. You'll be sitting with my mother, NeNe, and my sisters. I'm sorry your mother won't be able to join us."

"She said to tell you how proud she is of you. Business in Texas is good, and she's unable to get away. She said she'll watch the show on tv."

"I have so many roles in the show tomorrow, so I won't be able to walk the red carpet with you, and I probably won't see much of you until after the show. Will you be okay with Darien escorting you tomorrow?"

"Sure, it's fine." She kept her expression neutral to hide her relief. He was a media magnet, and she was glad she wouldn't have to face the pressures of the bright lights and the paparazzi on the red carpet. She never sought or wanted the attention.

"A glam squad should be here early tomorrow to help you and Darien prepare for the show. He's familiar with how things work, and he'll confirm their time of arrival with you." He hesitated before continuing and drew her chin up to gaze into her eyes.

"I won't be home tonight, but I'll be at the condominium downtown if you need me. We have dress rehearsals until late tonight, and I don't want to disturb you. Can I enjoy some lovemaking with you now?"

"You never have to ask for time with me. We're a team, aren't we?"

He picked her up and took her to their bed for an afternoon of love and fell asleep after giving her one last heart-stopping kiss. Still awake, she examined his hands while he slept. She had read all she could get her hands on about his genetic condition, but she was still curious about hands that could produce fireballs. He'd told her about his condition early in their relationship, but she had to admit, she still didn't understand the possibility of spontaneous human combustion.

She looked at his palms and turned them over to look at the back of his hands. He stirred a little but didn't wake up. She saw nothing unusual, and his hands felt like normal flesh. He moved his hand, and it fell out of her grasp, landing on her belly. She felt a warmth spread throughout her abdomen under his touch. His head bolted up off the pillow, and he withdrew his hand as if it was on fire.

"Are you okay?" he asked, his brows knitted together and his eyes blazed with concern. "What just happened?" He blinked his eyes, trying to reduce his confusion, and rubbed his hands for relief. She wished she could tell him, but she wasn't sure either.

"Get some rest." She cradled his head in her arms to settle him down. "You need to take a break before you go back to work."

He was tired and offered no resistance to spending quiet time with her before heading to practice tonight. They started the habit of enjoying a little downtime before he took the stage on the Fire God tour in Europe. They were in Italy when he told her that she held the power switch allowing him to turn it on and electrify the world with his high-energy performances. She knew how excited he was to share the stage with the saxophonist he'd idolized his entire life, his father.

He rested for a few hours before packing to leave for the condo downtown. Everyone left with him except for a skeletal crew of house staff and security to take her to the festivities tomorrow. For tonight, she wasn't going to argue about her need for a security detail; she had more important plans.

* * *

She took the bag of products she'd purchased earlier from the drug store, including a pregnancy test that she had shoved into the back of the chest of drawers to escape his prying eyes, since she didn't want to distract him before his big night. She went into the bathroom to see if her life would change forever and paced back and forth before opening the package and following the instructions.

I can't be pregnant, at least not now. We haven't been married a year yet.

He told her before he left that he was thinking about another tour and that he wanted her to go with him. She couldn't worry about that now. She took out the stick and waited for her answer after washing her hands. While biting her nails, she tapped her foot as if sending Morse code to the universe.

Please, not now. Please, not now.

* * *

The performers couldn't believe Miles wasn't obsessing over every move and every note at dress rehearsals. He was playful, lighthearted, and told the performers, "Let's have fun tonight. We may never get the chance to experience a moment like this again in our lives." He retreated to his dressing room hours before the show to FaceTime Bella. She told him she and Darien were enjoying their spa day and blew him a kiss.

"I have the passes for a reserved seat in the front row to catch all the action."

"Good." He turned his attention to a knock on his door. "I have to go. I love you. See you tonight."

"I love you too."

He hung up and yelled to the person at the door, "Come in!"

It surprised him to see his father come into the room, as he wasn't expecting him until an hour before the show. He gave Miles a big hug and looked around the room, which was full of primroses. Miles's contract rider was simple by industry standards. He demanded a heated room filled with primroses, to remind him of the Scottish gardens he'd toured with Bella, and bottles of water. Bosco, his German shepherd and collie mix, was free to go wherever Miles went.

"This has to be the biggest room back here." Cade turned to view the room again.

Miles shrugged and placed his hands in his pockets. "Have a seat, Pops. I wasn't expecting you until later tonight. Are Mami and the girls here?"

He sat down in the chair opposite him.

"No, I took an earlier flight. The girls are in school, and they'll be here later today. We'll be leaving early tomorrow so they can get back to school. I'm sure you remember the drill from the time when you toured with me."

"Those were fun but busy times."

"Yeah, they were good times. I heard your new songs: 'You,' and 'If It Wasn't for the Fire.' Son, you rose above the challenge I gave you years ago to make music that didn't contain the n-word, to drop the f-bomb sparingly, and to not live in a world inhabited by women you felt free to call bitches and hoes. All good music rises to a higher vibration, and larger numbers of folks will eventually listen to it. If you're lucky, your songs may add value to the genre. I wanted you to be a part of hip-hop's rising trends, to join the pantheon of hip-hop giants, but never forget to maintain your own voice. I'm proud of all you've accomplished, but tell me something, where did your edge and anger voiced in your music come from earlier in your career?" He leaned forward, his right elbow on his thigh as his left arm rested comfortably on the chair.

"Pops, your challenge was easier than you think. Hip-hop culture was already trending on a higher level, and the conscious subgenre of hip-hop is trending higher than ever. If you think of the options available to some young men, hip-hop offers an outlet for feelings of frustration and disillusionment. The music and dance industries are roads to legal entrepreneurship, and many of us give back to the community. I agree with you. The terms bitches and hoes are tired and overused in the club subgenre, but they use those derogatory terms once used to refer to only females now to refer to anyone, anything, and any place. A man who whines all the time is being a bitch, and something that is difficult is a bitch. Anyone can be a 'ho' if they diminish themselves for money in service to an idea or belief system, like some political hoes you see and hear on TV. We both know words like bitches and hoes are commercial ploys to get people's attention. I'm a self-made man and not new to the game. I don't have to resort to that kind of language."

He took a deep breath before answering the harder question about his anger. He had an enviable position of having a great father in a world where too many young people didn't know their father. Considering the possibility of his future as a father was his challenge instead of coping with life on his own without a father.

"Pops, you know I love you…and…I idolize you." He stumbled, but knew he had to continue. "I struggled with thoughts you deserved a better son than me…not some freak with a genetic condition who can produce fire." His expression hardened, his laughter deep and sardonic. "I know you and Mami had to go to great lengths to hide my burden." Fire appeared in the palm of his outstretched hand.

Cade rose out of his seat and paced as he searched for words to say. He suddenly stopped and turned in front of him.

"You're my only son, and I'm proud—do you hear me, son?—I'm proud and blessed to be your father. I've always been proud of you." Tears welled in his eyes as Miles remained silent and looked on, surprised by his father's raw emotions.

"Your mother and I wanted you to decide how to handle your gifts. We didn't want you analyzed by scientists, so we hid your talents as best we could to protect you, not because we were ashamed of you. We homeschooled you despite many offers to send you to schools for gifted and talented kids. We also kept your gift of fire a secret because we didn't want you blamed if an unexplained fire occurred. You wouldn't intentionally hurt anyone. Your internal fires purify a soul incapable of evil. The only two freakish things about you are your talent and energy level. I don't know how you do it. You're an entertainer to entertainers."

Miles got up and hugged his father hard. He had yearned for this conversation for years, but before Bella, he hadn't been able to find the words to express his feelings.

"I need to tell you one more thing." Cade hesitated. "We ran out of time while you were in New York, but better late than never. Here's the reality for five generations of Moore men: We all chose beautiful, fertile women who got pregnant early in our relationships."

Miles shook his head no.

"Don't fight it son; it's true. Look, Bella shares you with the world. Are you telling me you can't share her with three kids?"

He threw back his head, opened his mouth wide, and let out a hearty laugh. "Can you let me wrap my head around the possibility of one child before you bless me with three?"

"Alright, we'll start with one child at a time. Son, when you came along early in my career, I couldn't imagine how much fun it was going to be having my wife and my baby touring with me. It was the three of us against the world, and the time we had together made us unbreakable as a family—the perfect threesome. I wouldn't trade that time for anything in the world."

"Those were fun times, Pops."

"Just remember what I'm telling you." Cade looked at his watch. "It is what it is, son, and children are a blessing. I'd better leave now. I need to find my band members for our upcoming sound check and I'll see you in a couple of hours. You need time to relax before the show."

He rose and grabbed his father again. They stayed in an embrace as if years had passed since they last touched each other.

"I love you, son. Enjoy the show."

"Thanks, Pops…for everything. I'm proud to be your son, and congratulations on your Lifetime Achievement Award. You deserve it."

"Thanks, see you soon." Cade went to the door and closed it behind him as Miles turned his attention back to his music, humming the new arrangements to a song he planned to perform.

IF IT WASN'T FOR THE FIRE

Man huddled in Africa,
Sent prayers to the sun.
From earth's core,
Fire flowed, sparked the imagination
Of those who wanted more.

To remove the veil of darkness,
To heat up the night,
Destructive, constructive,
The spark of fire,
His greatest delight.

Fire cooked the food,
Fed the brood,
Sharpened tools,
A weapon in the hands of fools.

Man's greatest innovation
Gave birth to nations
Africans, Asians, Europeans, all others,
The original sisters and brothers.
Couldn't spread across the Diaspora,
If it wasn't for the fire.

Chapter Eight

YOU

You took the ember of my heart,
and turned it into a flame.
A passion burning deep within;
my life will never be the same.

Freed from the beast
that roared within me,
gone is my ire.
You changed me forever
with love and desire.

The fire of my passions
burns only for you.
I can't keep this secret any longer, babe,
what else can this man do?

You took the ember of my heart
and turned it into a flame,
of passion burning deep within me
my life will never be the same.

Ten minutes until the start of the show and Bella's auto alerts notified her there was an uptick of the song 'You.' There was also a message from her mother, telling her to enjoy the show. Seated between NeNe and Darien, she smoothed her pale blush pink strapless dress with the sweetheart neckline, reminiscent of a dress she'd worn to a formal dinner while on their honeymoon. She had reservations about the color of the dress, but Darien assured her only she could pull it off among a sea of black dresses on the red carpet.

She felt bold and fearless in the blush pink dress, her favorite color.

"You're at your best when you do you. If Miles wanted to see a black or red outfit tonight, he could wear it himself." Darien laughed while they waited for the show to begin.

She squirmed in her seat and straightened out imaginary wrinkles in her dress, unable to contain her excitement. She knew he would put on a good show, but still, she was nervous for him. This was their night, their triumph as a team. She puffed out her chest, so proud the star of the show was her husband.

The lights dimmed. "Ladies and gentlemen, I give you the incomparable, the one and only Ari."

He came out in his signature black outfit with army-style boots. The call and response between him and the audience was magical. Bella rose to her feet with the audience; the dance party had begun. She clapped and moved with abandon. This would be a night to remember, and she danced with the crowd, enjoying every moment.

She leaned over and spoke to NeNe. "He's in the zone tonight."

"Yes, he's putting on a great show, and the audience is with him." The entire front row sang along and danced with him.

She sat on the slow numbers and watched as her husband transformed himself into Ari, a phenomenal stage performer. There was no live fire in the theater, but he still brought the heat. He performed popular upbeat numbers but surprised everyone with a performance of the song 'You.'

NeNe looked over at Bella and whispered to her. "Miles provided 'surrogate' permission for you to be in the video," she said, enclosing the term surrogate permission in air quotes. "Try not to look shocked.

The cameras will be on you."

Bella jumped anyway, startled by the pictures of her lighting up the stage as he sang the first stanza. He came directly in front of her while the song's video showed her in a spontaneous dance with members of his crew. She held her breath as he shared an intimate and tender kiss between them with the world.

NeNe and Darien patted her hands, which she kept tightly wrapped around the arms of her chair. She felt exposed to the world as various images of her in a bathing suit, unguarded moments as she slept, pictures of him leaning over and kissing her cheeks, and moments of them alone in Italy flashed across the screen. She focused on keeping her back straight in her chair instead of shrinking down and disappearing in her seat. She peered into his eyes, the entry into his soul, and the riotous thoughts pinging through her head and threatening to send her into panic subsided. Without conscious effort, her thoughts became focused like a laser beam, sending and receiving only one message, *I love you and only you*. Her heartbeat slowed, and she squirmed less under his gaze.

He swayed on stage and didn't break his attention on her until she calmed. She loosened her hands from her death grip on her seat and raised them to her mouth to blow him a kiss. He winked and moved across the stage to sing to other members of the audience. Young women, including his sisters, screamed and jumped up and down when he stood in front of them. The song ended, and the stage lights went down. The broadcast went to commercial with the crowd applauding the performance.

The show continued, with other performers coming to the stage to perform or accept their awards. Miles returned to perform in the tribute to the hip-hop legend Jay Truth, dressed in a custom-made black tuxedo with a small pink rose in the lapel, and his father performed a number with his band before the close of the show. Miles joined them, wearing a fedora like his father, and took a seat with the band to play on the guitar the songs that once filled his home and his youth with joy. The set ended, and as he pointed to his father and the other band members, they received a standing ovation. The night was a success.

* * *

Bella said goodbye to the family members who planned to leave on the red-eye flight the same night back to New York. They had visited with Miles before the show started and told her they didn't have time to make it to their estate on this trip.

She had a personal escort to a waiting limousine, and she thought she was waiting for him, so they could go home to rest. She planned to wake up the next morning and share good news with him, at least she hoped he thought it was good. He had guards escort him to the limousine, where she showered him with congratulatory hugs and kisses.

"I'm so proud of you. You were fantastic tonight, and you deserved every award you won." She looked at the shiny statues while the guards placed his awards for Hip-hop Male Performer of the Year, Song, and Album of the Year in the car beside them. He loosened the tie around his neck.

"Thanks, baby. Sharing the show and the awards with you made tonight special." He took her into his arms and kissed her while rubbing her back and buttocks.

"I have some special congratulations waiting for you when we get home."

The car pulled off in the opposite direction of their home. She leaned away from him and looked out the window.

"Wait a minute. Where are we headed?" He took her back into his arms and snuggled for a moment.

"There's the afterparty we have to attend. You know I have obligations. Did I tell you, you look gorgeous tonight?"

"Thank you, and you're not so shabby yourself. Baby, you've been working nonstop. I thought we could celebrate alone at home and get reacquainted with one another, if you know what I mean." She sat up, pulled on his lapels, and showered him with more kisses.

"Place those plans on hold for now, baby."

She let out a deep sigh and pulled away from him.

"We'll have fun. This is your first time at an awards show as my wife, and I know you don't know what to expect at an afterparty, but the crew is waiting for us, and I'm sure you don't want to disappoint them, do you?" He pulled her back into his arms and laid kisses on her lips and down her neck.

"I guess not," she sighed again, with more determination to enjoy the moment.

The car arrived in front of the club and he pulled away slowly from her as he told her to put on the sunglasses in the door's pocket. She put on the shades seconds before the door opened to flashing lights. He exited the car first and extended his hand to escort her into the club. Loud applause erupted as they entered.

"Miles, I need to use the restroom." She spoke into his ear and he nodded, kissing him on the cheek before she left.

He headed for the bar, receiving congratulatory pats on the back from the other celebrants along the way. She saw Reagan and waved for her to come with her to the bathroom to freshen up. Out of the corner of her eye, she also saw Corey and Nadia seated in a booth as she headed out to the ladies' room.

* * *

Corey came to the bar to get drinks for him and Nadia and stood beside Miles.

"Congratulations." Miles nodded and turned his drink up to his lips.

"I've never been to one of these affairs before, but Nadia insisted on coming. You know her father owns this club, and she wanted to be here. She's talking to the audiovisual engineers right now." He chuckled. "She likes to control things and people."

He didn't answer Corey; instead, he nursed his drink. He thought the man still struggled with losing Bella, so he kept his eyes fixed on the bottles of liquor in front of him, trying to ignore him.

"We both know our women, Nadia and Bella, and what sweet lovers they can be...."

Corey jumped back in amazement as several candles, including the pillar on the bar between them, flared up. The flames danced just like a scene he had created in one of his shows.

"Whoa!" roared Miles's admirers, his gang of friends, and other performers.

"It's the Fire God!" they yelled. "The roof, the roof…." The crowd began to chant the old-school rap as the paparazzi captured the moment on cellphones and cameras before racing out of the club to upload video of the unexpected moment to their media sites.

"Listen, you little bitch," Miles responded, pointing his finger at Corey's face. "You need to stop thinking with your dick. Bella doesn't want you anymore. I accept you had a relationship with my wife, and I've had that freak Nadia on every surface imaginable, so why are we having this conversation?"

"You need not retaliate against me by lying about Nadia, Ari."

A picture of Miles staring off in the distance with Nadia kissing him on the cheek appeared on the big screens throughout the club. Corey stopped talking and stared at the pictures on most of the walls of the club. Stunned, he left his drinks at the bar to find Nadia.

* * *

Bella returned from the bathroom with Reagan, who held her hand tightly, pulling her toward Miles.

Reagan leaned over and whispered, "This is what I meant when I told you not to trust the bitch. She can't stand knowing she's on Miles's list as one of his castoffs and on Corey's list as a consolation prize. She's got to know Corey still has feelings for you. Her father owns this club, and I'll bet she had something to do with these pictures of her and Miles on the walls."

Bella, transfixed by the image of her husband sitting in a booth with Nadia, knew the photo had to be an old one. A television screen with a dated entertainment news show captured in the photo's background confirmed her suspicion. Lecia had shared her experiences of the games women played, and she now knew what she had warned her against. She wouldn't give Nadia the satisfaction of appearing jealous. Hell, she wasn't jealous. She encountered warm smiles from every woman she passed on the way to her husband while Nadia received a chilly response from others, including from the servers employed by her family as she passed through the crowd.

The DJ spun an old-school, throwback mix to get the crowd going. Bella was in the middle of the floor when the song "That's the Way Love Goes" came on. She crooked her finger to motion to Miles to come to her. The party crowd knew he didn't dance at parties or friendly gatherings, especially after a performance. He entertained others for a living, and he wasn't interested in performing when he was off. Everyone except Bella knew he didn't dance in public for pleasure.

She waited while he took a swallow of his drink before joining her for a brief sensual dance to the applause of others.

"Baby, I'm ready to go, but let's say our goodbyes and get out of here." He whispered to her.

"Sure, I'm ready too. It's been a long day." She took his hand as they made the rounds at various tables before returning to the waiting limousine. It was in the wee hours of the morning and she couldn't wait to get home. She dozed off on the way and woke up, yawning, as the car slowed and turned into the driveway.

"I'm going to hit the bed hard. I had fun, but I'm tired." She was still snuggled in his embrace, unaware of the sight unfolding before them.

"I don't think we're going to bed soon."

"What are you talking about?" She sat up and opened her mouth in dismay as they drove up to the front of their estate. Cars were parked up and down the driveway on both sides. She wasn't aware Miles had opened the estate to continue partying.

"You invited these people to our home?"

"Sure, it's better to party here and not worry about the paparazzi."

She rolled her eyes. When does this party stop?

Chapter Nine

Wide-eyed and initially frozen in her seat, she viewed the extended line of cars parked along the drive leading to the estate before flopping back in her seat, repeating the mantra: *It will be ok. This too shall pass.* She took in a cleansing breath and looked at Miles smiling and waving as he glanced out the window.

She always fancied herself the belle of the ball in her dreams. Her parties were always in ballrooms decorated in gold and yellow, and she allowed a smile to escape as she recalled her dreams of having many admirers. She'd been the unrivaled Yellow Rose of Texas in those dreams of so many years ago. The noise coming from people making their way to the house forced her back to reality, and her eyes misted as she looked out the window.

Don't fool yourself, girl.

Her reality had been different; she'd been the kid with few friends who wasn't invited to the parties among the popular set. She'd spent more time with her mother than with kids her own age. Even tonight, this wasn't her party. These well-wishers were here to celebrate Miles's success. Along with the songs from the Fire God tour, the songs "You" and "If It Wasn't for the Fire" were in the Top 10 and in a race to top the charts.

She took a deep breath as the limo came to a stop in front of the estate, and she resolved to make the most of the night. Putting on a happy face despite her fatigue, she willed herself to do all she could to be a supportive wife, sharing in the celebration of Miles's triumph as a leader and innovator in his field of music.

The limo driver opened the door of the car for them, and they got out, walking arm-in-arm to the front door, which Miles opened. Then he placed his hand in the small of Bella's back to escort her inside. As soon as the door opened, she was startled by the sounds of whoops and yells from his admirers. She resisted covering her ears to the deafening, unexpected sounds, which threatened to overwhelm her, and looked over at Miles, who beamed and waved with his left hand to all the partygoers in their home. He moved her to the center of the room with his right hand still resting at the small of her back and stopped at the center of the grand hall. With her in his arms, he began to sway to the sound of the music as he stared into her eyes and mesmerized her with his intense, loving gaze. He had a way of making her feel as if they were the only ones in the room, and even amid a crowd as large as the one gathered tonight, it was always just the two of them.

"I love you with everything in me. I'm so happy I can share tonight with you," he told her as they continued to sway to the music.

She noticed as she gazed at him that his eyes glistened under the bright lights, another sign of his anomaly. She knew in her heart it meant he was sharing a truth with her from deep within his soul. She peered into his eyes and placed her hands on both sides of his face.

"I love you, Miles, with all my heart, and I can't tell you how proud I am of you."

He stopped swaying and took her even closer into his arms. In front of all their guests, he placed one hand on her nape and the other at her lower back, just above the swell of her butt, and slipped his tongue in her mouth, kissing her deeply until she was breathless.

It surprised her how uncomfortable she was with such a public display of affection. She once thought she desired the attention of the popular set, but it paled compared to the joy she felt in the private and intimate moments she shared alone with him. Despite her current discomfort with the crowd of well-wishers who wouldn't leave, she wanted him to be with others who had played a pivotal role in his successes and had gathered here tonight to share the limelight with him.

She leaned against his shoulder, comfortable with the fact he loved her and wanted to acknowledge it to the world.

He surely proved it during his performance tonight.

She didn't feel he had to prove anything else to anyone, so she wondered about it as they danced.

Why his blatant displays of affection now?

"Drinks for everyone!" he proclaimed, breaking her thoughts as he loosened his embrace. The waiters came to offer drinks to them, and he drank up, beckoning her to drink hers after they toasted each other. Parker came up to them and caught Miles in a congratulatory embrace. Miles was engaged in conversation with Parker, which gave Darien just enough time to substitute her glass with a nonalcoholic drink. She'd told him about the pregnancy test while they'd prepared for the show and sworn him to secrecy until she had the chance to share the results with Miles.

"It's been a long day, and I know you're tired. This doesn't have alcohol in it. I looked at you across the room and saw you were fading. Take it; we'll talk later." He handed her the glass and took hers.

"Yes, Darien. I'm tired, and I promise we'll talk later," she whispered and held up her glass to sip her sparkling white grape juice.

"Get some rest as soon as you can. I'm planning on going into the office later today, so don't worry about anything."

"Thanks Darien. I think I'm going to sleep in after all of this."

"Catch up with you later."

He leaned in, embracing her before he left as she maintained a forced smile despite observing several women brushing up against her husband with their backs arched and their breasts pushed against his back. Yes, the room was crowded, but she thought there was no excuse for this inappropriate behavior. As she observed him, he seemed oblivious to their attempts to get his attention, but it didn't escape her awareness that other women were slipping bits of paper in his pockets as they came to hug and congratulate him. She decided she would hold her tongue. This was his night and his party. She didn't want to ruin it for him.

* * *

Bella observed Miles drinking more than usual, and she was becoming annoyed as he grew more amorous and sensual with her from the alcohol that unlocked what few inhibitions he had. She looked around at the party scene, which was becoming more raucous as the night progressed to the early dawn, with revelers displaying more humping between partners and twerking. The music playing throughout the house became more upbeat and driving in tempo. Miles came up, pulled her back on the floor, and danced.

At first, she stood in place as he danced around her as if he were saluting his queen, then she decided it was best to at least sway to the music, not wanting to be known as the party pooper. She wasn't about to attempt an intricate dance routine with all the professional dancers in the room. The song ended, and she whispered to him.

"Miles, I'm going to the bathroom." She pulled away from him and he kissed her again, unaware it was an excuse to escape briefly from his attention. Needing some air first, she headed for the kitchen, but a conversation in the hallway between two women who were making a wager stopped her in her tracks.

"I bet I'll get Ari in bed with me first," said one of the women.

The other cupped her breast and replied, "No, bitch, it's my turn tonight. All the money I spent on these double Ds, you don't stand a chance." She jiggled her breasts with both hands. Bella quickened her steps to interrupt their conversation before they got lost in the crowd.

"Both of you need to get out of my damn house immediately." She raised her hand to draw the attention of a nearby member of security. Her pulse raced and heat of anger flushed throughout her body as her own response to the women shocked her.

"Bitch, who you talkin' to? You must be drunk," the woman who'd bragged of her double Ds replied while the other woman whispered in her ear. They both pursed their lips and thought better of causing a scene, especially in front of a large man with burly muscles looking silently at them with his arms crossed over his chest.

"You're not enough woman for Ari," the more vocal of the two women continued.

Bella said nothing as they both gaped at her wedding ring with its large diamond dancing in the light. Bella stroked her chin with her left hand and contemplated how ludicrous it was for other women to cast wagers over her husband in her home.

The second woman approached within inches of her, and with a squint and a scowl, spoke up. "You're no better than the rest of us. You gave up the cherry too when it suited your purpose. Did you lie and tell him you were pregnant?"

Bella reeled back on her heels, and without contemplating her actions, slapped the woman's face. She covered her mouth with the same hand that had delivered the blow and took a breath to regain her composure. She didn't want the woman to see she had hit at her insecurities. Instead, she smiled as the security guard grabbed the women by the elbows and escorted them out the door.

"Get them out of here."

She turned away from them, held her tears, and headed to the back of the house. The cool marble kitchen counter felt comforting to touch as she leaned against it and took a deep breath, grateful for the calm, quiet space in the kitchen's corner. She knew there was something else she needed to do before retiring to the private suite with or without her husband.

I might as well do it now. She thought about it on her way back to the grand hall, still filled with the partygoers, and found him talking to members of the band.

"Can I speak to you alone?"

"Sure, babe, what's up?"

The others backed away to give them some privacy in the corner of the room. She placed her hands in both of his pants pockets and withdrew a fistful of small white papers and cards with names of many women in the room and their telephone numbers.

"Are these your afterparty invitations?"

He took the wads of paper and cards out of her hands and stared intently at them until a small fire appeared in his hands and consumed the papers.

"Look, Bella. Poof! They're gone."

She stared at the fire burning the little papers but not the skin covering his palm.

"Just like that, Miles?"

"Yeah, baby. Just like that and the problem is solved. You okay now?"

"Actually, I'm not. I'm tired. I'm going up to bed."

This nonstop partying isn't good for me or the baby.

She'd planned to tell him the good news, but they hadn't had a private moment together the entire day. She promised herself to tell him tomorrow.

"I know you're tired, Bella." He stroked the sides of her face. "I'll be up to join you shortly."

"That's an understatement. Goodnight." She touched her belly and kissed him goodnight before ascending the stairs to their bedroom.

Chapter Ten

He intended to join her upstairs in their private suite, but a band member detained him as he attempted to make his way up the stairwell.

"Leaving so soon, Miles? Man, all our hard work is finally paying off." He leaned over and whispered in his ear. "I got some good weed, but I ain't got enough for everybody. Let's go to your studio and enjoy this," he said, patting the bag in his pocket.

"Nah, man. You know I don't do drugs. I haven't touched the stuff in years."

"So what's been the source of your creativity?"

He shrugged but knew he owed some credit to Bella. She was his lover and his muse.

"Okay, suit yourself. I'm going to my crib if you change your mind. I'll save this baby for later." He patted the bag again before walking in the direction of the studio.

Miles turned and stumbled, feeling the effects of the alcohol. He rubbed the side of his face and looked to grab the railing along the stairs for support.

I deserve to drink to my success.

He smiled, the warmth of good vibes of success and being surrounded by people happy for him flowed throughout his body.

He knew he hadn't consumed this much alcohol in a long time, and he surely would not mix his alcohol with drugs. He stood and looked around at the others, who were also quite intoxicated. He had dreamed of tonight for many years and had secretly coveted the awards he'd won tonight. He wanted to be recognized by his peers, but despite his drunken buzz, he realized the fame and awards didn't compare with his good fortune of sharing tonight with Bella. Someone leaning her hands on his chest and taking his earlobe between her lips broke his thoughts.

"You've already tucked the baby girl in bed. Time for the adults to have some fun."

It wasn't common knowledge that Mya Kelly was one of his former, very experienced lovers and she once told him she loved the intensity of their lovemaking more than she had with any other man, including her husband. He hadn't seen her since his wedding day, and he thought he had made it clear he didn't want to reignite any of their passions from the past when they ended their relationship. He knew her well, and he guessed her presence at the party tonight signaled she didn't see his marriage as a deterrent to sex with him, but a mere inconvenience.

Even though he was intoxicated, he realized she wasn't about to desist in her attempts to pick up where they'd had left off several years ago. She moved provocatively in front of him, but he stood motionless, like a marble statue.

"Baby, I haven't gotten my celebratory dance with you," she told him as he stood, refusing to budge or cooperate in her attempt to drag him onto the dance floor.

In the past, this would have been a prelude to the rough and raunchy sex they'd often shared when he'd come off the road from a long concert tour. He had ended their relationship abruptly, and he wanted nothing more to do with Mya—not now, not ever. Somehow, she'd ended up with an invitation to this party, a celebration of his hard work, his dedication to his craft, and the belief of one woman in his talent—his Bella.

In the short time they'd been together, she had helped to expand his range as the entertainer who was being celebrated tonight. He was committed to her, and he owed her his fidelity. So many members of his organization also respected and cared deeply for Bella. He would never consider ruining tonight with a senseless encounter with Mya. He pulled her to the side so that others couldn't overhear their conversation.

"No, Mya. I told you several years ago, and I will repeat myself: There will be nothing between us again. Please leave now, and never return to my home."

Her head recoiled as if he had slapped her in the face, and her eyes filled with tears.

"Miles, please reconsider. No one could ever satisfy you the way I did," she told him. "We share a history. Your love once saved me."

He hissed as he responded to her. "I told you to never speak of our history. I never loved you, and what we once shared was a mistake. Remember: you signed a nondisclosure agreement to discuss no aspects of our relationship ever again. There will never be a time or place for us to discuss what we once shared. Mya, it's over and in the past, where it will remain."

She ran for the door, and he turned to walk away, dismissing further thoughts of Mya. He was relieved she left before he had Bradley or another member of security remove her. He didn't need another woman scorned and with reason to retaliate, possibly hurting Bella.

He saw Darien at the bar and raised his hand to wave him over.

"Let's go back to my office. I need to talk to you."

"What's going on Miles?" Darien wrinkled his brow and followed him as Miles stomped his way to the back of the estate and closed the door behind them.

"How did she get an invitation to my home?" The effects of the alcohol were beginning to dissipate as it evaporated under the heat of his anger.

"Did you know how much of a disaster it would have been if Bella saw she was here?"

Darien opened his mouth to answer the barrage of questions coming his way, but another question came his way before he could answer, so he sat back in his chair.

"I thought you checked over the guest list?"

"I didn't tell Bella about the party here tonight, and she would have assumed *I* invited Mya and *I* wanted her here. After Mya crashed our wedding, Bella would have handed my ass to me in a sling and she would have had every right to do so."

He paced the room, not realizing Darien hadn't answered any of his questions but was observing him walking back and forth in this moment of self-reflection.

"We've got to get our act together, Darien." Then he stopped and turned to face his executive assistant who, over the years, had become a close friend.

"No, I've got to get my act together, and I'm going to need your help. Before the end of this week, I want you to change all of my contact numbers, my account numbers and limit the security access to a very few individuals. You and I, and Bella of course, can have a meeting to discuss the list and to make sure she's alright with it."

"Sounds like a plan." Darien got out of his chair to fist bump with Miles.

* * *

This is Miles's world.

She looked back at the crowd, uncertain if she had a place in his world. She got to their private suite, closed the door, and a knock came at the door before she could take off her shoes.

"Is Li'l Pharaoh in there?" Li'l Pharaoh was one of Miles's young protégés.

She opened the door, her patience running thin.

"Why would he be here?" she asked the young woman standing before her.

"I've searched the entire house, and I can't find him. Do you know where he went?"

"No, I don't. Now, please leave, I'm tired."

The woman rolled her eyes and responded, "Okay, Queen Bee."

She closed the door and drew her fists tightly in balls as her body shook uncontrollably. Something had snapped inside her—a rage she didn't want to visit on a stranger.

I've got to get out of here. This isn't my home. It's Miles's home and his party.

She packed a few things in her suitcase and took the back stairwell past the kitchen and out the back door.

"Bella. Bella, please stop. I need to talk to you." She turned her head to the sound of a familiar voice and faced the woman who had crashed her wedding.

"What do you want, Mya?" She closed her eyes and slowly opened them as she looked upon this woman whom she hated to admit she was beginning to loathe. She didn't know the history she and Miles shared, but she had heard the gossip, and she figured it was probably a sordid tale.

"Leaving so soon, Bella?" Mya peered at the suitcase.

"Why are you concerned about anything I do? And why are you at my house?" She responded as she eyed her from head to toe, her lips curled in disgust.

"Well, then let me be brief. I'm here to help you. You probably heard that Miles and I share a past that I'm not ready to end."

Bella placed her suitcase on the ground as beads of sweat popped up on the bridge of her nose.

"You're not from around here and you may not know we share our good fortune with others around here. I won't be greedy, but I'm letting you know I will be sharing some time with your husband, if you know what I mean."

Bella gathered her fists at her side.

"So, you're asking if I'm alright with you sleeping with my husband?"

"No, I'm telling you girl, out of respect for you. You can't be that dense."

The same hand that had been itching from hostility landed across Mya's cheek, causing her head to sling to the side.

"If it's not me, it will be someone else." She railed and placed her hand against her reddened cheek.

"Get out of here before you get the butt whipping you've been asking for." She lunged forward as Mya turned and ran toward the parked cars.

The muscles in her arms quivered as Bella wiped away tears.

"I've had enough of this. I have to get out of here."

She looked around and hurried to the limousine that had brought them home from the awards show and was still in the driveway. She tapped on the window, and when the driver got out of the car, she gave him the address to her childhood home. She needed rest and to get away from the madness of Miles's world. She looked at her reddened hand as it began to swell.

"Maybe I do need security to protect other people from me. I've done a lot of witch slapping today." She sighed and sat back in her seat as the car traveled down the driveway.

* * *

Miles was in the main hall about to head upstairs after talking to Darien when Bradley approached.

"Miles," he whispered, "I just got a call from the limo driver. Bella had him take her to her old place on Vermont Avenue. He made sure she got inside safely, and he's gonna stay and keep an eye on the house."

"I know I'm reversing myself again but, tell him to get out of sight. I haven't had the chance to tell her I reassigned a security detail to her. Does anyone know why she left? Did something happen?" He searched Bradley's eyes for answers as many questions ran through his mind.

"Is she all right?" He placed a hand on Bradley's shoulder.

"I don't know the answers to your questions, Miles. All I know is that she asked the driver to get her out of here."

"Take me to her now!" he demanded.

That she'd left him had a sobering effect. He wrinkled his nose from the smell of the alcohol mixed with sweat coming out of his pores and assaulting his senses. His heart was beating frantically, the blood coursing through his veins burned with fear and the remaining effects of the alcohol in his system evaporated. He followed Bradley to his security car and his heart thumped, pounding in his chest as he sat back in his seat, anxious he may have already lost her.

They maneuvered their way through the busy streets of LA, trying to avoid as much traffic as possible. Miles had a set of keys to the home on Vermont Avenue for security reasons, and after Bradley unlocked the front door, the house next door blew up, knocking them both to the ground in front of the house.

The chauffeur who had driven Bella to the house came running toward them and helped them as they staggered to their feet.

"The garage door is open and there is a Mercedes parked inside it. I saw a woman slumped over the steering wheel and was about to check it out when I saw the two of you." He grabbed both of them under their arms.

"Bella doesn't have a Mercedes. I'm going to check out the house." Miles had made it to the front door before a second loud rumble and flash of fire roared in the garage of Bella's home, rattling the house. Sirens blared in the background as the fire spread to the front of the house. Bradley shielded his eyes from the flames while Miles kicked in the door and ran through the home, looking for her.

"Bella!" he yelled as he ran through the bright red and orange blaze and disappeared in the haze of black smoke.

Chapter Eleven

"It's too dangerous! You need to get out of there!" Bradley yelled. "Come back! The house might blow again, and we should wait until the firefighters get here."

Miles ignored the warning as Bradley backed away from the burning door and he moved forward, knowing Bradley would alert the firefighters to the fact he was inside the house looking for Bella.

The front area burned out of control as Miles called out to her, but she didn't answer. He was wild-eyed with fear he wouldn't find her.

"Bella!" he yelled out as he shielded his eyes from the flames. Drenched in sweat as he raced from one room to the other, he looked up and saw the fires burning hot yellow and orange mixed with black smoke coming from every room down the hall, everywhere except from her bedroom.

"Bella, where are you?"

His heart beat frantically, and his vision narrowed with each passing minute. He ran down the hall to her bedroom in the rear of the house and saw her lying unconscious on the floor.

"Bella! Oh God, please help us."

He rushed to her side and felt she had a pulse, but her breathing was shallow. He threw an object on her nightstand at the window to break the glass, and the sound of the glass breaking drew the attention of the firefighters now on the scene. Flames came into the room as he scooped her from the floor and ran to the open window, delivering her to safety. He grabbed the treasured photos of her as a little girl with her father in front of his motorcycle and a few other photos before escaping through the window with the help of the firefighters. He got to the sidewalk just before another explosion occurred, destroying her beloved home and her mementos of the past thirteen years.

He insisted on riding in the ambulance, which sped through the streets with his unconscious wife. He heard the sirens of other ambulances and overheard one of the two emergency responders tell the other a natural gas leak in the neighborhood was the suspected cause of the tragedy. He located his cell in his pocket and called Bradley.

"I'm on the way to the hospital with Bella, and thanks for your quick thinking. If you hadn't alerted me, I wouldn't have known she had left the mansion and I might have lost her," he choked with emotions. "One more thing, please call my parents and Joan so they won't worry, but you don't need to take shit from my father. Tell him to save it for me."

"I'll call them now. Bye Miles."

She was still unconsciousness but alive and breathing. He held her hand.

I can't lose you, he thought as he wiped a tear away with his sleeve.

"She's breathing on her own, but she's not coughing despite the amount of smoke she inhaled, and neither are you." The EMT furrowed his brow and drew his lips. "I guess that's a good sign, but highly unusual. Sir, if I could ask you some questions, it will save some time and help the team in the emergency room. How do you know her, and can you tell me what happened?"

"I'm her husband, and I arrived at the house just before the explosion. My security team alerted me she was inside and...." He broke down again and tried to compose himself before continuing to speak to the EMT, who turned away to watch the monitors while Miles gathered his thoughts.

"I found her unconscious on the floor in her bedroom and got her out of the room with the help of the first responders." He stroked her hair, but she didn't respond to his touch.

"Is there anything we should know about her physical condition? Could she be pregnant and does she have any medical problems?"

"Her blood pressure has been high in the past, but she said it was under control the last few times she had it checked, and she has environmental allergies and...." *I've had enough sex to impregnate her.*

"No, she's not pregnant," he answered, despite knowing it was possible with their recent inconsistency with birth control.

He saw the EMT raise an eyebrow following his hesitant response to the question.

"We're newlyweds, and I guess it's possible."

He kissed her forehead, and her eyelids fluttered as he whispered her name.

"Bella, sweetheart. It's Miles. I'm here."

She opened her eyes briefly before turning her head to the side and closing her eyes. She didn't squeeze his hand; instead, she tried to pull away from him. The EMT closest to her stayed busy, looking at the monitors and checking her vitals. They arrived at the emergency room, where they rolled her into an exam bay for assessment.

His phone blew up with messages, but Miles only answered the call from his parents and told them to meet him at the hospital.

"The girls are on a flight back to New York with NeNe," Lecia told him on the phone.

"But we're still in town and I told Cade we should stay overnight in Los Angeles. I was concerned about Bella before the fire because she looked so tired and pale after the awards show. We're on our way to the hospital and should be there shortly."

"Thanks, Mami. I'm in the waiting area in the ER and I should be here unless they move her."

"We'll find you Miles. See you soon."

"Bye Mami. I love you." He choked up again.

"Bye son. We love you and Bella too."

He placed a call to Bella's mother, who had just left the country to attend the International Fire Safety Conference with her clients from

Texas. She had many questions, but he didn't have answers about Bella's condition yet.

"I'll be on the first flight out of London. Bye, Miles."

"Bye, Joan." He hung up the phone and tapped his foot, agonizing as he waited for someone to come out and tell him about Bella's condition.

* * *

"Miles!" His parents rushed to his side and hugged him after they arrived in the emergency room to sit with him while Bella underwent testing and stabilization. The charge nurse finally came out and assured him they would allow him to see her as soon as possible. It concerned them that Bella's blood pressure had dropped precipitously just after they'd arrived in the ER, and she also acknowledged she had a word with some newly hired junior staff who became starstruck when they saw him roll into the ER accompanying his wife. She placed Miles and his parents in a private room next to the emergency department to await the news about Bella, and she assured them they would maintain her privacy.

"I've called in a specialist to consult on her case," Cade told him. "We need to cover all the bases and make sure she gets the best care."

Dark circles formed under his eyes as he waited for further news. His mother distracted herself with magazines in the room while Miles and his father stared off into space.

"Son, I'm glad you told Bradley to call us. I want to let you know I apologized to him for my behavior while you were touring in Europe. I know he and his security team did a great job protecting you, but I've never heard of so many credible death threats against an artist, and that shit scared me. It's also hard to remain objective when the person threatened is your son."

"I appreciate it, Pops. Bradley's doing a good job despite the limitations we've placed on him. He doesn't know about my anomaly."

The doctor came into the room to tell them Bella didn't require a trip to intensive care. Miles introduced her to his parents, and she took a seat to brief them on her care.

"The EMT gave us a report she wasn't pregnant, but her tests have confirmed a pregnancy. You needn't worry at this point. I've called in an internist, and they will involve an obstetrician in her care."

He looked back at his parents with a slackened jaw and hollow eyes. He couldn't find the words to describe the pit forming in his stomach, while his parents were both nonplussed and sat impassively in their seats. He wondered if they were in shock. Neither one of them offered words of surprise or support.

"We'll answer more of your questions after we get you back there with her. Please follow me to see your wife while they're getting a room ready for her on a general medical floor."

He got up and followed the doctor in silence.

"We'll be here waiting for you. We love you," he heard his parents say to him as he disappeared out the door.

* * *

Miles was on his way back to the waiting area to get his parents after a brief visit with Bella when he encountered Cade coming out of the bathroom.

"Miles, let's talk before we go back to see your mother." He guided Miles over to an empty consultation room.

"Bradley told me what happened over at Bella's family home, and I became concerned it was a planned threat against her life."

Miles sat back in the chair as he braced himself while Cade pulled up a chair.

"What are you talking about, Pops?" He gazed at his father with a laser-like focus despite his fatigue. "Who would want to hurt Bella?"

"Hear me out son. I've run this past the operatives at the Network and we're all in agreement: if someone wanted to hurt you or get to you, Bella would make the perfect bait. There's also the issue of the woman found in the garage who died in the explosion."

"Pops, I can't hear this, okay?" He turned his head and fought back the tears. "I'm too raw to hear that it was because of me, Bella is struggling for her life. I can't do this right now."

"There's nothing you have to do right now son. I'm just telling you that the explosion tonight has caught the attention of the Network and they're investigating it. I thought you needed to know."

"Thanks, Pops." He got up, placed his hands in his pockets, and stood facing his father.

"I need to focus my energy on Bella right now and seeing her through this. I know you spoke to me before we got married about the need to keep security around her, but I wanted her to be happy and not frustrated that she was living in a fishbowl, and I didn't listen to you. I'll never forgive myself if I lose her. I won't."

Cade came closer and hugged him.

"I'm not here to tell you I told you so, son. I'm here as a man who has been in your shoes before and I know your pain."

Miles grabbed Cade in a tight embrace and in the privacy and anguish of the moment, he sobbed like he hadn't done since childhood.

Chapter Twelve

I WAS BLIND

How could it be?
I just couldn't see
that the pleasures of your love
are a gift from above.

Why couldn't I feel
my spirit rise,
as I gaze
upon your beautiful brown eyes.

How could I not hear
the rhythm of my heart
beating stronger, faster
whenever you're near.

I took for granted
the taste of your sweet lips,
the warm caressing touch
of your fingertips.

The scales fall off my eyes
as I realize
I was blind
but now I see.

Miles and Cade went back to the waiting area where Lecia was waiting for them.

"There you are Cade. Is there more news, Miles?"

He knew the turn of events frightened her, and she rose as they entered the room and immediately peppered them with questions.

"Is she all right? Is she awake? What did the doctors say?" He motioned for all of them to sit down as he took a breath and ran his hand through his hair.

"Her blood pressure has stabilized, and she's resting comfortably. She opened her eyes briefly when I called out her name, but they told me she was exhausted and would probably sleep for most of the day. They took her to her room upstairs, and I came back to get the two of you."

"How are you, son?" his mother asked, and his father nodded out of concern.

"I'm all right, just worried about Bella…and the baby."

"We didn't want to share our feelings about a new baby since it was clear you didn't know she was pregnant. We felt you needed time to embrace the idea yourself, and that's why we remained silent. You need to know, however, your mother and I will do anything to help you. We're elated to have a grandchild, and we're here for you." His mother nodded and wiped the tears from her eyes.

"When can we see Bella?" she asked.

"You can see her now. I came to take you to her room upstairs."

They gathered their things and accompanied him to the elevator to get to Bella's room. She was asleep when they entered, and his mother went to her bedside, wiped her eyes glistening with tears, then placed her hand over her mouth to muffle her sob. Miles looked first at his mother standing across from him and then cast his gaze back on Bella.

He was initially numb in the ambulance and in the ER with Bella, and as if gaining clarity on her current condition for the first time, he stopped and took a long look at her through a lens darkened by sadness. His mother took Bella's limp hand in hers and began to stroke it.

"Bella, sweetheart, it's Lecia. I'm here with Cade and Miles. We love you."

Bella didn't respond to her mother-in-law's gentle strokes and soothing words.

Miles's eyes glistened as he looked at her, pale and seemingly smaller under the sheet on her hospital bed. It frightened him to see her looking frail, and he reached for her other hand and kissed it, then bent forward and kissed her on the lips. She stirred at his touch and struggled to open her eyes but seemed to find the bright lights in the room disturbing.

The nurse came in, checked her IV bag, and lowered the lights before leaving them together.

"Bella, it's me." He took a seat by her bedside. "Mami and Pops are here, too."

She moved her head, and her eyelids fluttered again, but this time, she opened her eyes and looked at him. She swallowed hard and tried to speak.

"Where am I, and why am I here?" she asked softly.

"You're in the hospital. Do you remember anything from this morning?"

She shook her head.

"Do you remember going to the awards show last night?"

"No," she told them.

"What about the trip to your childhood home?"

She started to cry and shook her head.

"I don't remember much about yesterday." She sobbed and held her hands over her eyes.

He ran his hands through his hair and decided he needed to proceed slowly with her.

"Sweetheart, do you know who I am?" He held his breath.

"Of course, you're Miles, my husband, and they're your parents."

She pointed to Lecia and Cade.

He let out a sigh of relief and kissed her again on the lips.

She tried to sit up, and he assisted her by repositioning the pillows against her back.

"What else do you remember, Bella?"

"I remember feeling angry, I don't know, maybe frustrated and overwhelmed; I'm not sure which one. It tired me out, being surrounded by too many folks; people were talking in the kitchen about Parker saying he couldn't stay long to party with them because of his family tying him down and something about you and other women. It's all hazy. I'm not sure what happened."

Miles and Cade shared a brief knowing look before they turned their attention back to Bella.

"You attended several parties last night with Miles, the social butterfly," Lecia told her. She leaned over and gave her a hug. Bella returned her embrace, then touched her belly under the covers.

"I remember I haven't told you something very important." She hesitated before continuing and grabbed both of his hands. He felt the pressure of her grip tightening and looked at her, waiting for the news.

"I'm pregnant, and I've suspected it for a week. I tried, but I couldn't find the right time to tell you."

He didn't respond right away but looked up at the wall despite knowing she was looking at him and searching for his response.

"The doctors told us already."

He said nothing further for a few seconds as he struggled to find pleasing words for her benefit. He refused to lie or pretend he was happy about the news.

"I'm processing the news," he said, lacking enthusiasm.

Her countenance dropped. He sensed she read his response as a sign of the conflicted thoughts he couldn't hide from her. She knew him too well, and he didn't resist her attempts to pull her hands away from his loose grip as she turned to Lecia for comfort, leaving him feeling powerless while he watched her crying and her shoulders convulsing in her emotional pain. His shoulders drooped, as he knew he had disappointed her, and he placed his hand on her back, rubbing it and trying to soothe her as best as he could.

"Please, don't cry," he pleaded with her. "You know I can't handle your tears."

She calmed as his mother held her and struggled to console her. Cade answered the phone ringing his pocket.

"Yes, I see." He said little as he listened to the person on the other end of the call.

"Alright, I'll get back with you soon." He ended the call and proceeded to tell them the nature of the call.

"Friends of mine knew of the work of a Dr. Chancellor, an expert in his field who has privileges at this hospital, and he agreed to consult on Bella's case. He's on the way up to share the results of his findings."

Bella wiped her eyes and stopped crying after Cade told them the news. Miles got on the bed and was relieved she allowed him to cradle her in his arms. They braced for the news as the door opened and Dr. Chancellor entered.

Lecia and Cade rose from their seats to greet him and shook hands. Then he extended his hand to Bella and Miles.

"I have good news," he told them. "Bella, your tests look good. Your oxygen saturation levels are good, and there has been no damage to your lungs. I've been studying the genetic anomaly Miles shares with a few others around the world for years."

"What about my baby?" Bella asked.

"Yes, Dr. Chancellor. What about our baby?" The doctor looked at Miles and then turned to face Bella.

"My colleagues examined you before I arrived and reported to me you're farther along than was first suspected. We performed an ultrasound and discovered two gestational sacs, about five weeks along. It's possible two more people share your condition, Miles. You and Bella are having twins."

"Did you say twins?" Their voices echoed throughout the room.

"Yes, twins," Dr. Chancellor reiterated. "It's possible that one or both of your children share Miles's protein structural changes. This protection, passed to you, Bella, from one or both of them, allowed you to withstand the high temperatures in the fire without burning your skin. It also allowed you to buffer the negative effects of smoke inhalation. It will take time to be sure if they both share these traits."

"So, you're telling me, Dr. Chancellor, my children saved my wife's life?"

"I'm saying the traits you passed to them protected Bella and she'll have this protection while she's pregnant with them. There is a high likelihood she could have died or been in the ICU, fighting for her life right now." Miles hugged her, drawing her closer to him.

"Doctor, please tell me. Are my babies going to be okay?" She sought reassurance again.

"They look good on ultrasound, Bella. I'll explain the ramifications of their genetic condition later, after you get out of the hospital. If there are no more questions, I need to finish my rounds and return to the lab. I'll be available by phone if you need me."

He said goodbye and left the room. Cade and Lecia followed him outside to give Miles and Bella time alone.

"Did you call my mother?" She looked up at him while he stroked her hair.

"Yes, she's on her way from London. She's coming straight to the hospital from the airport as soon as she arrives."

"Thank you. I need her, but why was she in London?"

"The firm she was under contract with decided at the last minute to send a delegation to the International Fire Safety Conference, and Joan was selected as a delegate."

"Oh, I see." She leaned against his chest.

"I'm sorry if I disappointed you, Bella. I should have seen you were too tired from the touring, the parties, and the demands of my lifestyle. I'm sorry I put my needs above yours, and I'm sorry I'm not more excited about the babies. Wow, it blows my mind to say babies, but I'll get there." He ran his fingers through his hair. "Nothing is more important to me than family. I see things more clearly now. Please be patient with me. I would have died if I lost you."

"I forgive you. You've only had minutes to get used to a reality that took me a week to absorb. I should've told you sooner. The possibility of your rejection frightened me, and I didn't get a pregnancy test until two days ago. I could have insisted we make time to talk, but I needed time to deal with my own feelings. You know some will say I got pregnant on purpose to trap you."

"I could have been more honest with you. I've struggled with the idea of passing this thing I have to our children, and that's why I've been conflicted about having children. We've talked about wagging tongues before, and we've also decided to let people think what they want to think. We can't worry about it."

He stretched out his right hand, and a fireball appeared in his palm.

She waved her fingers across the fireball, and it didn't burn her skin. Her jaw dropped as she looked at her fingers unaffected by the heat of the flames. Her ringtone, "That's the Way Love Goes," played on her cell phone placed on a nightstand by the staff. Someone had found the phone undamaged in her pocket the night of the fire. Distracted by the flame burning in her husband's hand, she didn't answer the phone right away as it continued to play the ringtone.

"I'm blinded by my love for you, like a butterfly mesmerized by flames," she told him as he looked at the screen and grabbed the phone ringing beside her bed.

"I think it's your mother on the phone. You should answer it."

Miles watched as she took the phone from him and steadied herself with deep cleansing breaths before speaking to her mother.

"Yes, Mom. Miles told me you were on your way from London and I'll see you later today."

She nodded as she listened to her mother.

"The doctors were optimistic about my recovery, so please try not to worry about me. I love you too. Goodbye Mom."

She smiled and ended the call on a cheery note, but Miles knew behind her brave facade was a woman still shaken by a terrifying turn of events. A burning discomfort settled in his stomach as he recalled seeing Bella on the floor of her bedroom surrounded by smoke and fire.

The fire in his belly slowly burned away as he looked at her, grateful that she was safe.

After her brief conversation with Joan, Bella tried to make small talk with him, but her eyelids grew heavier from fatigue, and she fell asleep in his arms.

In the last twenty-four hours, he had gone from feelings of sheer terror to feeling a warm glow of solidarity with the woman he loved more than life itself, who now shared his genetic gift even if it was only for a short time during her pregnancy.

He lowered them on the bed and leaned his head back on her pillow, falling asleep with his strong arms holding her and their babies in the cocoon of his protection.

* * *

Bella was still asleep when Miles tipped out of the room in response to a text from his father with the room number and a request to meet him in a room on the same floor but at the end of the corridor.

"Yeah, Pops. What have you heard?" He yawned as he walked into the room.

"I have some answers, but I have more questions. It's looking like the explosion was an accident as a result of a fractured gas line and not a nefarious attempt on Bella's life. The body found in the car in Bella's garage was badly burned, but the authorities identified the vehicle and confirmed the body was Mya Kelly." Miles stumbled backwards and he had difficulty drawing in a breath as his chest tightened under the weight of the news.

"Let's have a seat, son. I need you to tell me everything you know. Why was Mya at Bella's home? The security feed at the house showed that Mya drove her car to the house and parked it in the garage after Bella entered through the garage and left the door up."

Miles rolled his eyes as his head fell back against the chair.

"I don't know why Mya went to Bella's house. The last time I saw her was at the party I had at the estate last night. We got into an argument and she left."

"Well, Miles, let me say I don't believe it was a coincidence that first, she travels to Scotland to come to your wedding at the last minute, and then she shows up at your wife's home with Bella in the house alone. What was going on between you and Mya?" Cade remained calm as he crossed his leg during what appeared was the beginning of an interrogation.

"What the hell, Pops? What are you insinuating?" Miles raised up in his chair as if poised to pounce.

"Careful, son. You're getting all defensive, and I haven't said much of anything. Now tell me, what was going on between you and Mya?"

"I'm sorry, but it feels as if you're accusing me of something I didn't do." He sat back in his chair as his chest heaved and he rubbed his chin, contemplating his answer.

"Nothing has happened between me and Mya for years."

"Alright, that's a good start, son, but what happened between the two of you in the past? Miles, please, I need to know."

He sighed and looked at his father as Cade's gaze didn't waver despite the growing silence. Miles cast his eyes at the floor before looking up and answering the question.

"I had an arrangement with Mya…and her husband Donald."

Cade turned his head and placed a finger behind his ear as if he was having difficulty hearing Miles.

"Excuse me, what did you just say? An arrangement with Mya and my friend Donald?" He knitted his brow.

"You heard me, Pops. Mya was ten years younger than Donald, and I guess he didn't please her." He paused and blew out a deep breath.

"This is hard, so let me finish."

Cade didn't listen and opened his mouth to speak. "Mya was fifteen years older than you, I think. Hell, she babysat for you. Miles, how could you?" he asked through gritted teeth.

"As you said, you and Mami brought her into *my* life, so who's at fault here?" Miles returned a verbal volley, hitting Cade square in the chest as he watched a pall of sadness descend upon Cade, who placed his hands on his head and rolled it from side to side in anguish.

"Why didn't I see it? I felt something was off, but I just didn't want to go there."

"I did a lot of things I'm not proud of, but I've learned from them. I was a young man in my early twenties, and you and Mami had returned to New York when Mya came to me with a proposition after she seduced me the first time. No, she didn't assault me, and yes, I willingly had sex with her and I knew it was wrong. I wasn't going to let it happen again when she came to me and told me she told her husband Donald about what happened between us. He wasn't angry about it, she told me." He swallowed hard as he struggled to maintain eye contact with his father.

"Go ahead, Miles. I'm listening, and son, I'm working hard over here trying not to judge you, so tell me the rest."

They both rubbed the back of their necks, aware the stress of the news was a burden for both of them.

"Donald was into this strange shit at the time and he was okay with Mya kicking it with me as long as we agreed to a schedule and limited the sex to only the days on the schedule."

"What?" Cade popped out of his seat and began pacing like a caged tiger. "That bastard. He was my friend and I helped finance his music studio as a silent partner and that's how he repays me? He involves my son in a sick threesome?"

"Yeah, Pops; he liked coming in afterwards and having sex with Mya when she wore the scent of another man. Of course, Mya and I didn't stick to the schedule and one day he surprised her and came home early from a business trip. Mya called me and I could hear him yelling at her in the background. I went over there, and by the time I arrived, he had beaten her and she was covered in black and blue bruises. She came to the door, and I went in to intervene and that's when he tried rushing me. I only wanted to warn him, so I threw a fireball in his direction that landed in the fireplace, but he tripped and fell, hitting his head on the marble slab in front of the fireplace. He was out cold, and I begged Mya to call the authorities, but she pushed me out of the door and told me she would handle it. The next thing I'm finding out like everyone else watching the news of a fire at their home and the firemen couldn't save Donald, who died in the fire. She told the authorities that they were fighting and he fell into the fireplace, setting the house ablaze. Hours later, I get a text from Mya telling me to say nothing. The sex between us continued for a few months and then I broke it off. I told Mya we weren't good for each other and she needed to get help. I hadn't heard from her until the day of my wedding."

Cade resumed his seat and they both sat in silence as Cade absorbed the gravity of Miles's confession. He looked at Miles and asked his last question.

"Did you love her, Miles?"

It didn't take long to answer the question. Miles knew love and fidelity within a marriage were important to his father.

"No, Pops; I never loved her. There was a lot of good in Mya, and it pains me she had to die the way she did. It just seems ironic that she bore the burden of the truth of her husband's death and she also experienced a death by fire."

"The irony of it wasn't lost on me either, son." He placed a hand on Miles's shoulder.

"You know I'm going to have to share this with you mother, and she's going to be devastated by the news. There was a time when there was a lot of affection and respect between those two women. I'm going to have to tell her the news of Mya's death and the truth about what happened between the two of you."

"I understand, and I knew that when I made the decision to tell you. Pops, I need to get back to Bella."

"Yes, of course. I'll speak to your mother and I'll leave it to you to decide how and when you share it with Bella."

"Thanks Pops, but right now, I don't feel Bella needs to bear the burdens of my transgressions. For now, I'll continue to bear them on my own, and whatever I need to do to protect Bella and the babies are my only concern at this time." He looked down at his watch.

"They should be moving her to another room today and I need to get going." He began moving toward the door.

"I'll catch up with you later, Mijo." Cade waved goodbye and Miles stopped and smiled before placing his hand on the door.

"It's been a long time since you called me Mijo. It felt good hearing that again."

"It felt good saying it again. Tell Bella your mother and I will be in to see her later after you all have gotten her settled."

"Okay. I need to check and see if a more spacious room has come available." Miles opened the door and walked the long corridor to the nurses' station before returning to Bella's room.

Chapter Thirteen

Bella blinked, struggling to get her bearings as she awoke in a larger, unfamiliar room with plusher surroundings. Her mother was asleep in an oversized chair at her bedside, but she awakened to her stirrings.

"Hello, my sweet girl. Are you feeling better?" Joan stretched her arms and rose to kiss her daughter. She stroked her hair just as she had done to comfort her when she was a little girl.

"I leave for a couple of months and come back to find out you're pregnant and my house burned to the ground." She rolled her eyes and let out an audible sigh, feigning exasperation.

"Mom, don't play with me. What do you mean the house burned? Our home is gone?"

"Yes, Bella, it was completely destroyed. Don't you remember? They suspected the explosion happened when a gas pipeline fractured."

She cried. Sad and overwhelmed, she didn't filter her thoughts and fears.

"Where will I go, Mom?"

Joan's eyes widened, and her posture stiffened.

"What do you mean, where will you go? Is there something you're not telling me?"

"Mom, Miles's lifestyle overwhelmed me so much I needed to

retreat. Even when we're in our private suite of rooms, there are knocks on the door, cell phones always ringing—the noises were constant."

"Bella, I can answer the question for you," Miles told her as he walked into the room and hugged Joan before kissing Bella.

"Hello, Chief. I'm glad you're back. Bella needs—no, correction—we both need you now." He joined them, sitting next to her on the larger bed. She looked to the side and saw the familiar picture of her and her father on the nightstand. She figured Miles must have rescued it from the fire.

"We can rent the house next to ours if you'd like. My parents spoke to the owners, and they agreed to a rental lease for a year. It will give us time to decide if we want to build on the adjacent property next to our current home or come up with something different. I want you happy and at peace. Our children need a healthy environment—starting now. We can decide on the rental together after you have time to tour the home. I think you'll like it. The rental house is a smaller one-level home."

"Are you serious?" She looked at him, hardly containing her grin, and placed her arms around his neck.

"I love you, Bella Moore. I'll do anything for you and our children." He placed his hands lightly on her abdomen. This time his eyes were brighter, and his voice cracked with emotion.

"Your happiness means the world to me too, Miles. We should move to the neighboring house close to your studio. I think it's the solution to our problem."

She smiled at him, happy to be surrounded by the people she loved most in the world: her husband, her babies growing in her womb, and her mother.

"Children?"

"Yes, Mom, we're having twins."

* * *

After her discharge from the hospital, Miles and Bella had settled into the rented home near the studio. He had returned to work, and she chose to accept few visitors to ensure she got some rest, but today, she was looking forward to a visit from Darien.

She was sitting in one of the outside rooms overlooking the hills decorated with lush greenery and a large fountain gurgling in the background when Darien came to join her at the table.

"Hi, Bella." He came over and kissed her.

"Please don't get up." He loosened his embrace and gave her the present he brought.

"I wanted to be one of the first to congratulate you."

"Thanks, Darien; but you shouldn't have." She looked at the present, covered in brightly colored paper and wrapped in pink and blue bows. Her belly had begun to protrude, and there was no mistaking she was pregnant.

"Looks like you've been busy growing your latest project." He made an image of a large semi-circle in front of his abdomen as Bella laughed with him.

"I'm not that big, at least not yet." She gave him a side-eyed glance. "Please, have a seat, and thanks for coming."

"Girlfriend, you've been sounding a little sad on the phone lately, and nothing would have stopped me from coming over to check on you. What's going on?"

A member of the house staff came outside and placed their lunch plates in front of them.

"Thank you, Ned." Bella addressed him before he departed. They ate a bit of food before Bella responded.

"Are you worried about Miles's writer's block? It's true he hasn't been able to compose anything since you got home from the hospital, but it's happened before."

He placed more food in his mouth and listened.

"I wasn't aware he was having a problem at work. He hasn't said anything about it."

"Well then don't tell him I said anything about it. So, if it's not that, what is it?" He placed his fork on the table beside his plate and looked at her.

"Something else has been gnawing on me and I need to ask you about it."

"Tell me. What is it?" He wiped his mouth with a napkin on the table and gave her his full attention.

"You've been Miles's executive assistant for years, and you know more about his past than I do so…I need to know, has he ever asked you to arrange a threesome for him?"

He cleared his throat and coughed into his napkin. "Excuse me, but wouldn't you know if he was involved in a threesome? You, him, and someone else? Oh, I forgot, it would be more than a threesome, you, him, the twins and someone else?"

She rolled her eyes at him and blew out a breath.

"You're so nasty and if it was possible to be a relationship where you loved and disliked a person at the same time, that would be you and me." She pointed to herself and then to him.

"You know what I mean. Has Miles asked you to arrange a tryst for him with two other non-pregnant females?" She struggled to swallow the lump in her throat as tears gathered in the corners of her eyes. He took her hand tenderly in his.

"I knew we would have this conversation sooner or later, especially after you told me you saw the sexual fantasy videos he had on his phone." He sighed and then continued.

"You're the best girlfriend I've ever had, and you know I love you, but Bella, I can't get in the middle of you and Miles. He's my boss and he deserves my loyalty. I've thought about this since the two of you got married, and it's probably for the best that I find another job. I love both of you and I don't want us all to get caught up in a tangled mess."

She shook her head with vehemence, staring at him as the tears began to fall.

"No, no way. You can't quit, and I promise I'll never place you in a compromising position again. I just didn't know who else I could ask about this. I'll get it together." She took her hand out of his and wiped away her tears.

"Bella, someone has dropped something in your spirit."

"What do you mean by that?" She dried her eyes.

"My mother used to say that when I would obsess about the things others would say about me, and believe me, I've had to work through a lot of nasty and negative things thrown my way. She would tell me to forget that shit before the weight of the words sunk into my spirit and became a part of what I thought about myself."

"Oh, so you think I'm listening to others?" She blinked as she tilted her head and considered if there was some truth to what he was telling her.

"I don't read the tabloids and I'm off social media?" She questioned if those things were the source of her distress.

"I know you don't, and I think it's something more personal. Someone has led you to believe you're not enough for Miles and there will always be someone threatening your marriage, but even if you weren't my best friend, I would tell you unequivocally, if Miles didn't meet and marry you, he would be a single man for life. I don't know if you're aware of this, but Miles has been given an example of fidelity in marriage by his father and uncle. He believes in fidelity, and that's why he once thought he would never marry. He used to enjoy the nightlife, but I haven't seen him so happy as he looks forward to being a family man."

"Really?" She smiled at him.

"Really Bella. I don't speak from experience but, I hear pregnant women get hormonal and you're carrying twins so maybe that's the case times two."

"Thanks Darien. I feel better. I'm glad I shared my thoughts with you but, don't worry about it. I don't plan to make you my marriage therapist. That wouldn't be fair to you."

His phone buzzed and he looked at the message on the screen.

"I've got to finish some things back at the office and you should finish your lunch."

He got up and went to hug her as he prepared to leave.

"Don't get up. I'll see myself out. Bye Bella."

"Bye, Darien. I love you." She waved goodbye and watched him as he stopped in front of the glass door and turned to face her.

"He never asked me to arrange a threesome for him. Never."
He walked away without saying another word.

* * *

Miles returned home after a long day at work and Bella had just changed into a new outfit after finishing her bath filled with lavender and vanilla scents. They were in the den watching television after enjoying their evening meal, and he had a small drink and a glass of flavored water with a twist of lemon waiting for her before she came in to join him.

"Bella, I've been trying to find the right time to talk with you about this, and I've decided there is no right time. I know we've talked about this before, and I need to be honest. I've reinstituted your security detail." He rushed the words out before his resolve faltered.

"I see." She frowned as she thought about her next response. "You've been so busy worried about me. Is that why you've been stuck in a creative drought? You haven't been spending time in your office, and you haven't been showing me your new compositions. Is there a reason why you feel I need added security? What's really going on?"

He moved closer to her on the couch and kissed her, rubbing her belly at the same time.

"Bella, there are no active threats against you or me, and I know you don't want to be surrounded by security, but I was scared as hell after your house caught fire in that explosion. An investigation was launched, and the findings were consistent that it was an accident after a gas line was fractured. I lost a lot of sleep worrying it was a planned attack on you, and I guess that's why I haven't been creative. There's just the usual communications from fanatics who tell me if they can't have me, no one else will."

He took her into his arms as she snuggled against his chest.

"It's alright Miles, and I know in the huge volume of mail you get, some of the messages can be disturbing. Do whatever you need to do to keep me and the babies safe. I'll adjust to having a security detail." She tried to pull away, resigned to the fact that her life was about to become more complicated.

"Please Bella, I don't want to fight about it." He let out a deep sigh and held her tight.

"Didn't you hear me. I said it was alright." She was trying to be agreeable, but she couldn't hide the edge in her voice as she looked ahead and avoided his eyes.

> *"I don't want us,*
> *to do this,*
> *I don't want to fight,*
> *No, my Bella, not tonight.*
> *You're the apple of my eyes,*
> *My eternal delight.*
> *With you, I'm mesmerized,*
> *by your glow in the evening light.*
> *No baby,*
> *I don't want to fight.*
> *No, my love,*
> *not tonight."*

He sung the melody softly in her ear as he nibbled the tip of her earlobe.

"You're not above manipulating the situation to get your way, are you? And you're not fighting fair." This time she smiled and leaned against his chest.

"I'm not trying to manipulate the situation, but I've thought long about it and I think I've come up with a compromise."

She looked up at him and waited for him to share his plan.

"What do you think about this?" He stroked her cheek as he told her of his plan.

"Instead of a convoy, what do think about having Jaimie MacGregor, the guy assigned to you in Scotland, come over and be your personal guard? He has a unique skill set of experiences as a former member of his country's special forces, as an anti-terrorist expert in evading capture, and he was once a stunt driver. He has agreed to a job promotion in our organization by guarding the people who mean the most to me: you and our babies. He likes working by himself or with a very small amount of staff."

She rubbed his arm as she listened to his proposal.

"I think that could work, but you have to agree to start taking care of yourself by eating more. You've lost weight for every pound I've gained." She smiled and touched the side of his cheek.

"I'm worried about you, Miles."

He laid a kiss in the palm of her hand.

"Don't worry about me, but I can't eat or sleep knowing you're over here while I'm next door at the estate surrounded by security. Okay, we'll both need to compromise." He smiled at her.

"That's not all, Mr. Moore. I have additional terms."

"Let me get comfortable while I listen." He got up and stretched out on the couch, placing his head on her lap.

"I feel like a weight has been lifted. I'll agree to anything if you let us harden this home with more security. I need to feel you're safe."

"As I said, I'll agree to your terms if you stop looking at me through your telescope when I'm doing my yoga practice in the morning. It's not relaxing being observed all the time."

She had on a cotton and spandex yellow top that draped over her belly and a matching skirt that was gathered midthigh as he lay with his head on her lap.

"You can see me looking at you?" He looked under her top and kissed her swollen belly.

"I can see the reflection of the sun bouncing off the metal cylinder and I know you have a telescope in your office. Instead of looking at me, why don't you get back to work and start turning out some compositions? You're going to miss deadlines and we won't be able to release the next album in time."

"How do you know so much about what's going on at AriMusic? I thought you were getting rest. Sounds like Darien has been talking too much again."

"Well, while we're talking about Darien, let me confess something else. I asked Darien if you had asked him to arrange a threesome for you."

"He told me about the conversation you had with him, and at first, I was angry you didn't come to me with your concerns, but I know you and Darien are close." He sighed.

She placed one hand in his and pleaded with her eyes as she turned his head so that his eyes met hers.

"Darien and I will never be as close as you and I are. I'm sorry, and I made a mistake by letting my fears get the best of me, but I can't believe Darien shared my concerns with you."

"He knew you would tell me eventually, and he also knew you would be angry with him, but he said you loved him and would eventually forgive him. With me, not so much. He thought I wouldn't take the possibility of a betrayal very well."

She rolled her eyes as she listened to him talk while he peeked under her skirt.

"Someone must be putting thoughts into your head that I want someone else. I don't know what else to do. I can give you all the passwords to my cellphones and all my social media accounts if you want." He looked under her skirt again.

"I already have that information. Remember, I was your public relations person on the Fire God Tour?" Her mouth slackened as she tilted her head to the side. "I know I shouldn't worry you're surrounded by skinny, scantily clad women during rehearsals but, I'm sitting over here with my belly swelling more every day." She patted her foot on the floor.

"Isn't that a good thing? It means our babies are growing and that's what we want, right? Besides, working with women is a part of my job, and I chose to marry the woman who had her clothes on. Well, you had on underwear the day I married you, but today, you're sitting in a short skirt with no drawers on. If you're trying to turn me on, it's working."

He winked at her.

"Stop looking under my skirt and don't try to change the subject. I know you have to do your job, but it doesn't make me feel better knowing you're surrounded by temptation."

He leaned forward and kissed the skin on her inner thigh.

"Since you're so curious about why I haven't been wearing underwear lately, I'll tell you what's going on. I've been so hot carrying these babies, it feels better not wearing panties."

He took in a breath and then blew a puff of cool air through his pursed lips on her exposed clit, sending shivers up her spine and causing the muscles of her core to tense and heat with lust.

She thrusted her pelvis, releasing a burst of ecstasy and threw her head back.

"Oh Miles, that felt so good." She bit her lip and lowered her head to kiss his lips.

"Why are you doubting my commitment to you, Bella? You know there will never be anyone else. There's only me and you." She was stroking the side of his face and stopped as the memory of her last conversation with Mya returned.

"What's wrong, Bella?" He looked at her as her eyes widened with the realization of the effects Mya's words were still having on her.

"I'm not sure if this happened, but I think I got into an argument with Mya at the estate before I left. She told me that you wouldn't be satisfied in a monogamous relationship and I needed to accept there would always be someone else in our relationship. I think she was trying to convince me that you will have an affair sooner or later." Her body heated with anger and her pulse raced.

"Is that all you remember?" He sat up and took her into his arms.

"That's all I remember." She didn't resist his attempts to calm her by rubbing her shoulder and laying kisses on the crown of her head.

"I don't know about all that went down between you and Mya, but there was security footage from your home that showed Mya followed you to your house. She parked her car in the garage just prior to the explosion and she died there."

Bella leaned up and searched his eyes.

"Why would she follow me, Miles? What else did she need to tell me that was so important to her? Whatever it was, she paid for it with her life." He lifted her chin so that he could look at her. The pained look in his eyes and the heaviness in her chest caused an initial concern about her ability to hear and deal with the truth of his relationship with Mya.

"Mya and I shared a past beyond being family friends. It was over with long before I met you." He opened his mouth to continue, but she placed a finger to his lips.

She realized in that moment the choice was hers.

Do I want to be burdened by the actions of a dead woman? She's no longer a threat to our relationship. She searched her heart for the words to say.

"It was over and now she's gone. I don't need to know any more about it."

"But Bella, I don't want you to hear anything about me from anyone but me."

"Who else is invested in telling me about you and Mya?" He looked into his mind's eye for the answer.

"No one, I guess." He waited for her response.

"It's done and settled then. I've put my fears to rest and we move on."

"Bella, it will always be just the two of us. My wish to find the woman of my dreams was fulfilled when I found you." He smiled at her.

"My three wishes were granted when I found you, Miles. I wanted a man to love me for me. I wanted our marriage to be happy as we grow older together, and I wanted to be the mother to your children."

He took the back of her hand and laid kisses on it.

"Your three wishes are granted, my Queen. You are my treasured Madonna with child. It blows my mind seeing our babies grow inside of you, and the sex with you, oh my gosh. You've been so wet and delicious. Sometimes I'm sitting at my desk craving the sight of you and longing to be with you."

"You can relax now knowing that we're safe and I'll be here

anxiously awaiting your return," she reassured him.

"You drive a hard bargain, but it's one I can live with. You stop worrying about me and I won't worry about you. It's settled." He lowered his head and kissed the fullness of her breast.

"I love how your body is changing and becoming so soft and even sexier than ever."

"You have a way with words, and I'll expect to see some lyrics soon."

"You're my muse baby, and I promise I'll get back to work, but first, I need to finish this conversation in the bedroom where I can talk to you in private."

"You want to talk?" She gave him a side-eye look.

"Talk, and some other things." He helped her to her feet and placed his arms around her as he guided her to their bedroom.

* * *

A personal office was set up at their home so that she could assist with the marketing of the new album. Bella liked the privacy of their temporary home, with its spectacular views in the hills of Los Angeles. She and Miles got opportunities to sit uninterrupted by business demands and enjoyed looking at the sunrises in the still of the early morning, and if they were lucky and he got home in time, they witnessed the vibrant sunsets in the evenings together.

She didn't go to the studio too often during her pregnancy, and she had only a few visitors during the first weeks after her discharge from the hospital. He limited his work hours to be home with her at night, often lying at her side and marveling at the growth of her belly containing their twins.

The new album, *Fire of Love,* shipped platinum with three solid hits. Bella enjoyed observing the process, the creation of a song from Miles's drafts to the collaborations with others who provided the beats and musical arrangements. Slowing down his schedule gave him more time to write.

Miles told her his father once shared an old saying: "As long as the lioness can't write, it's the hunter who tells the story." It inspired him to put more time into developing the Vesta division of his company, named for the goddess of fire, since he had a desire to bring more female voices into the hip-hop music industry.

Latifah Elliott, Myoshi Matsui, Brit Taylor, and his principal dancer, Reagan Madison, who was also a good singer, were the first artists signed to his new division. He planned to introduce them in an extended version video of his song "Four Sisters" and eventually produce his first hip-hop opera—a hip-hopera.

Bella and Miles enjoyed their days together as they eagerly awaited the birth of their twins, whom they already showered with their love and attention.

MILES ARIDIO AND BELLA ALIYAH WAHLBERG MOORE
ANNOUNCE THE BIRTH OF THEIR TWINS:
MILES ASHTON (ASHE) MOORE 5 POUNDS 13 OUNCES
AND
RAVEN ARIANA (ARIANA) MOORE 5 POUNDS 1 OUNCE
ON
SEPTEMBER 2ND

The twins were born on the same day the album *Fire of Love* went multi-platinum. Setting up the Vesta division of AriMusic had kept him busy during his hiatus the last nine months, and he decided against signing on for a tour during his children's first year of life.

Ariana looked like her father, with her mother's temperament, while Ashe looked like his mother, with his father's temperament. Miles and their nannies attended to the twins when Bella needed to exercise or get a break.

"I don't want you so exhausted that you have no energy left for me, nor will I compete with my own children for your time and affection. My mother recommended a distant cousin come to help us, but I know you've got your heart set on another woman you interviewed who bonded well with the babies, so let's hire them both," he told her days after they brought the twins home.

"Well, we'll always have a back-up helper if your cousin wants to go back east for a visit and we don't have to worry about burning her out taking care of two babies. But two nannies, Miles?"

"You could hire three if that's what it takes to make sure we resume our sex life as soon as possible."

"So you're thinking with the other head again?"

"Yes Bella, and I'm not apologizing for it. We can afford the help, and I think it's important to maintain an active sex life. I grew up surrounded by a large extended family who took care of me and loved me. I want the same thing for our children." He looked her in the eye, and Bella knew he would not back down from his position.

She had to admit, having help allowed her time to start a home marketing business focusing on inventions by stay-at-home moms and to continue to give time to the Moore family charities as often as she could while taking care of the babies.

They decided to build a private home on the land next to their studio estate. They scheduled the house to be finished in a little more than a year, barring delays. Bella liked that the location allowed maximum views of sunrises and sunsets. Miles joined her sometimes for her yoga practice, and she couldn't be happier as her twins thrived with love and attention from their extended family.

He told her she'd inspired him to write "Four Sisters" after he'd observed how well she got along with the diverse group of women in his organization, especially since she didn't have sisters.

"I realized a long time ago that, in the human family, the females are all sisters whether or not we like it," she told him.

One year later, he proudly accepted the award for "Four Sisters" in the category of Video of the Year: Long Version. He and Bella skipped the afterparties and went home to their children immediately after the music awards show to enjoy a private celebration.

FOUR SISTERS

A mystery,
the history, of
Man and Woman Kind.
The parents of four daughters,
greater beauty and grace,
you couldn't find.
Four sisters,
Africa, Asia, Europa, and America.

Africa, the oldest of them all.
Blessed with great strength and might,
toiled the land from sunrise to sunset.
She wouldn't stop until her work was done.
Harvesting food with hands that blistered,
she would do anything for her sisters.

Africa had hopes and dreams,
hopes that sprung from the heavens above.
A hope that one day, the family of Man Kind,
would have many children to love.
Precious gifts of boys and girls,
living happily throughout the entire world.

Man Kind however sadly knew
that a darker day would come.
He prepared his daughters as best he could,
with the gift of fire and the second gift,
A drum.

                    Michele Sims

You're the smart one.
The pretty one.
The strong one.
To each sister, others would say.
Sowing seeds of dissension,
creating a terrible atmosphere of tension
between the four sisters,
Africa, Asia, Europa,
 and America

Man and Woman Kind
kept Africa at home.
To foreign lands, the others roamed.
The younger three sisters were sent away,
too much envy among the sisters
Asia, Europa and America
sadly, couldn't stay.

Africa was promised many children,
lands of diamonds, oil and gold,
but nothing could comfort her
after she was told.
Her sisters were sent away
Asia, Europa and America
couldn't stay.

Africa's tears gave rise
to rivers and oceans.
She couldn't fathom the notion
of life without her sisters.
Heart sad and heavy with grief,
she no longer felt the fires
of her hopes, her dreams,
of her true desires.

She couldn't see that fire
would light the way.
A sign from Europa, Asia, and America
to forever say,
We love you Africa,
We'll be together again, someday.

Asia took her fire,
Added artistry and flair,
To light up the skies
with fireworks that sent sparks
far and near.
With fire, she created incense and spices,
fiery and hot
to tickle the senses of traders
who came to the East
to taste her exotic treats.

Europa took her fire
to shape metal tools,
and fashioned great buildings of wood and stone.
She built imposing structures meant not for her glory alone.
Africa once told her of a great Creator,
the giver of all good things.

The One whose breathe gave her life,
the Deity who made her.
Europa was so inspired
She created great hymns for others to sing.

America, the most precocious of all,
took her fire and
under pressure created tall buildings of steel.

Hidden in her gift of fire
was a great seal.
A seal of duty
so great she could feel
that someday she would be a beacon of hope.
A new home,
a promise to all her nieces and nephews
with warm embraces and open arms,
none of whom she would ever refuse.

Time passed by,
the sisters grew old.
Hearts of men
grew hardened and cold.
Africa decayed, her children sold,
to the children of Europa, Asia and America.

In the midst of chaos and confusion,
some heard the beat of the drum.
The second gift from Man Kind
to his children who had become
guilt ridden, downtrodden
by wars, by famine
by love of mammon.

Misplaced priorities,
the pride of life,
placed on a pedestal too high
to hear the pain and sufferings,
or the children's cries.

Despite it all,
beat drummers beat,
for resurrection of souls,

for restoration of higher goals.
Beat drummers to reclaim
the revered name
of the Egyptian Goddess,
the wife of Osiris,
the mother of Horus.

Now is the time
to remove all things
children of Man and Woman Kind.
Things that impede the love,
an abiding and undying love
of four sisters,
Africa, Asia, Europa,
and America.

Thank you for reading my book, *A Moore Affair*, the fourth installment of the Moore Family Saga. If you enjoyed reading it, please do me a favor and leave an honest review where you purchased it.

The first three books, *Act I. Seed on Fire, Act II. Playing with Fire* and the third book *The Fire God Tour* are all available on Amazon.

Sign up at michelesims22.com with your email address for updates and giveaways and join us in the Author Michele Sims Group on Facebook.

Your support is appreciated.

Michele Sims

is the "author-ego" of Deanna McNeil and creator of the Moore Family Saga. She loves writing hot love stories and women's fiction with multidimensional characters in multigenerational families. She is the recipient of the 2019 RSJ Debut Author Award, 2018 RSJ Aspiring Author Award, and first runner up in the Introvert Press Poetry Contest for February 2018. She is a member of BRAN, LRWA, in Charleston, SC, a former member of the From The Heart Romance Writers' online group, SC Writers' Association, and RWOWA.

She lives in South Carolina with her husband who has been her soulmate and greatest cheerleader. She is the proud mother of two adult sons and the auntie to many loved ones. When she's not writing, she's trying to remember the importance of exercise, travelling, listening to different genres of music, and observing the wonders of life on this marvelous planet.

Facebook Author page- https://www.facebook.com/michelesims2122/
Newsletter- https://michelesims22.com/
Instagram-https://www.instagram.com/michelesims2123/?hl=en
Twitter-https://twitter.com/dmichele2123
Bookbub-https://www.bookbub.com/profile/michele-sims
Amazon-https://www.amazon.com/Michele-Sims/e/B07KPVCMKG/ref=ntt_dp_epwbk_0
Goodreads: https://www.goodreads.com/author/show/18618421.Michele_Sims
Website- https://michelesims22.com/
Email- michelesims2122@gmail.com